DOUBLE DOWN

JUSTICE OF THE COVENANT: BOOK TWO

M.R. FORBES

Published by Quirky Algorithms
Seattle, Washington

Cover illustration by Geronimo Ribaya

ACKNOWLEDGMENTS

THANK YOU to YOU, for picking up the second book in the series. I hope you like it as much as the first.

THANK YOU to my beta readers and editors. I could never do this without you.

THANK YOU to my wife. I could ABSOLUTELY never do this without you.

HAYLEY OPENED HER EYES.

Every once in a while, when she was tired enough or had been in a deep enough sleep, she forgot that the action didn't have an equal and opposite reaction. No light filtered in through her pupils. No detail formed ahead of her retinas. As always, there was either darkness or color. Rainbow paints shifting and turning against a matte black canvas.

It was the same as when she was asleep. Her mind had learned to settle into it when she was tired, accepting the physical closing of her eyes as a signal to drift away. That was when the rainbow patterns could really go wild. That was when they formed into dreams and memories. All of the ones she had known before going blind had been converted. She could hardly remember what the world looked like anymore.

When she was tired enough or had been in a deep enough sleep, the realization of that simple truth was as painful as the healing wound across her side where Bale's claws had reached through her lightsuit and left three deep gashes.

There was no Medical Bay on board the Chalandra. No

med-bot to put her back together. She had been forced to settle for the Colonel stitching her up, the way he had stitched up his face many years ago, a repair job that had left him with nasty scars under his mechanical eyes.

She could barely remember what she had looked like as a child anymore. And she had no idea what she looked like as an adult. She knew she was in good physical shape, but that was because she was highly trained as both a doctor and a soldier. Did she have a pretty face? She didn't know. Normally, she didn't care, but she had woken up too fast, and a sudden sense of vanity crept through.

The scars were ugly, and more than just visually. They would be a forever reminder of her first combat drop, and how shitty it had all turned out. Her foster-mother was dead. Her mercenary family, the Riders, were almost all dead, save for her and Colonel Quark.

And the bitch that had betrayed them.

She knew the traitor was a human woman, one of five on the ship besides Nibia: Sykes, Damonze, Lattimer, Noab, or Li. She had described them to Tibor, but he hadn't been paying much attention to what any of the Riders looked like, and some of them were so damaged they were hard to identify anyway.

Whatever. They would be reaching Augustine soon. Hopefully, they would get some answers there.

She shifted in her bed, forcing herself not to fall back to sleep. They had taken the Chalandra as payment for helping the residents of Kelvar get rid of the Nephilim. It was the most expensive starship in the fleet of five ships that had landed on the planet. A billionaire's pleasure cruiser, appointed with the most luxurious crap in the universe. The bed was so damn soft and warm and comfy that it was making it hard for her to keep her daily ritual. She had overslept twice already, and now she was groggy as all hell.

"Get up," she told herself, focusing her sense of vision. She grabbed her visor from beside the bed and slipped it on.

"Good morning, Witchy," Gant said.

"Good morning, Gant," she replied. "How long until we drop?"

"Seventeen minutes, twelve seconds," the AI replied.

"Frag. What time is it?"

"Eight fifty-three Earth Standard."

Had she overslept again? "Damn it. Quark's going to be pissed."

"Is Quark ever not pissed?" The AI chittered in amusement.

He had been even more pissed since Kelvar. Not only had he lost his on-again, off-again wife and lover in Nibia. Not only had he lost most of his crew. Not only had he been captured once; he had been captured twice in the span of hours. It was a matter of pride that was sticking hard in his craw and making him more difficult to deal with.

And he was rarely easy to deal with, at least for most individuals.

She was a partial exception.

She managed to pull herself out of the deep cradle the bed had made for her, standing on a thick, cloud-soft rug and padding across the bedroom to the living quarters of her private suite. A large screen graced the forward wall beside the door. A ridiculously comfortable sofa faced it.

A serving-bot powered on and started rolling toward her.

"I don't need anything," she said, waving to it and turning left into the bathroom.

She turned on the shower, enjoying the sound of the real water splattering on the floor. Then she pulled off her undershirt and panties, climbed in, and spent thirty seconds in wet bliss while she washed herself clean.

She was dressed and into the short corridor on Deck A, headed for the bridge, five minutes later.

"Good morning," Tibor said, joining her in the hallway as she passed the intersection leading to the ship's fitness bay. The Goreshin was recently showered and dressed in civilian clothes, just like her.

"Good morning, Tibor," she replied. "I like your pants."

He laughed, knowing her well enough by now that he knew she couldn't make out the detail of his pants. The only reason she knew she wasn't completely mismatched was because Violent had done the shopping and organized the outfits before they had left Kelvar.

"I like your, well, everything," he said feebly.

"Did Violent do a good job?"

"I believe so. I missed you at practice."

"I know. I'm sorry. I overslept again."

"The beds? Ugh." His qi turned reddish in slight anger. "I can't stand them. I've been sleeping on the floor. You should, too."

"With any luck, the Colonel will flip this ship for something more suitable when we get to Augustine."

"With any luck that isn't yours, you mean. With your luck, the ship was stolen, and we'll be arrested as soon as we hit the dirt."

"Don Pallimo will have taken care of any registration clean up that needs to happen before we get there."

"Is he really going to meet us there?"

Hayley nodded, even though she was lying. The founder of the Crescent Haulers had died years ago, but few people knew it. The current Don was a neural network built from the original's brain. His physical stand-ins were fakes; incredibly expensive bots made to look like what most people thought he looked like, which also wasn't the real thing.

It was a lot of misdirection, but it had to be when you were one of the most powerful individuals in the galaxy.

"He promised Quark he would come personally. He doesn't consider the Nephilim attacking the Riders a direct assault on him, but he and Quark are as much friends as anyone can be, and he has no love of the Nephies. He'll help us get back on our feet and back after those assholes."

"I can't wait to meet him."

"You don't have to wait much longer."

They finished making the trip to the bridge, taking a plush stairwell to Deck B and moving near to the bow of the starship.

Quark was standing next to a ridiculously thick and plush command chair, which was draped in white leather and what looked like diamonds. He turned as they entered.

"You're this close to being late," he said.

"Sorry, sir," Hayley said. "I overslept again."

"Damn beds," he said. "You should've grabbed the floor, Hal. You don't want to get soft."

"I know. Tibor suggested the same thing. You both should have talked more sense into me three days ago, not ten minutes before we dump out in Augustine's orbit."

Quark laughed. "Damn right. Nobody but myself to blame. Tibs, take the pilot's seat and get ready to guide us in. Witchy, take nav. You know, because you have to sit somewhere."

She moved to the navigator's seat, while Quark flopped into the command chair. He shifted around on it uncomfortably, cursing under his breath at the soft leather.

"It's kind of hard not to go soft on this ship, isn't it, Colonel?" she asked.

His qi shifted gray and sad. "Every time I go to sleep, all I see is Nibia and the Riders."

5

She felt herself tense at the response. And here she was sleeping too much.

Everybody grieved in their own way. She took it out on Tibor in the fitness bay. She had reopened her stitches twice already. She probably shouldn't have been pushing that hard, but Quark would never be the one to tell her to dial back her effort.

"What's the plan once we touch down, Colonel?" she asked, getting as far away from the subject as she could.

"There should be a Hauler waiting for us in-system with a message from the Don," Quark replied. "It'll provide instructions on where and when to meet him."

"I'm surprised he chose a Republic world instead of an Outworld planet."

"Me too," Quark admitted. "I'm sure he has his reasons."

They spent the next nine minutes in silence, waiting patiently as the clock counted down. When it neared zero, Tibor shifted in his seat, reaching for the Chalandra's controls.

"Ten seconds to drop," a pleasant male voice said.

"It'll be nice to get this shit moving forward again," Quark said. "I hate twiddling my fragging thumbs."

"Roger that," Hayley agreed.

"Three. Two. One. Disengaging disterium drive."

The Chalandra had been moving faster than light through suspension in the gas of a crystal known as disterium. A containment field held the gas around the ship while it moved them partially out of phase with the universe, enabling them to break some of the oldest laws of physics in the galaxy. As the mechanism that produced the gas shut down and the containment generators turned off, the ship 'dropped' back to sublight speeds, emerging from the blue-tinged haze.

Hayley couldn't see the universe beyond the transparency

separating the bridge from the vacuum of space outside. All she saw was the bridge through the filters of Quark and Tibor's life energy, and black detail where the windows sat.

She didn't have any trouble hearing though, and the immediate shrill tone of warning that blared around them told her instantly that their luck was still hers.

And it was still shit.

"Frag me," Quark said, hesitating for only an instant. "Tibor, evasive maneuvers."

Hayley knew from the sudden inertial forces that Tibor was already executing, adjusting the vectoring thrusters and the main engines to move the ship out of harm's way. She felt the pressure against her stomach, grabbing for the emergency belt and pulling it over and across her chest as she buckled in.

Something exploded right near the ship. There was no sound to it, but she could feel the vibration on the hull from the oxygen and gas evacuating the warhead.

"Who the frag is shooting at me?" Quark said. "Tibs, what have you got?"

"A fragging mess, Colonel," Tibor replied. "It looks like they baked us a cake."

"What?" Quark asked.

"Uh, they knew we were coming," Tibor said.

The g-forces pulled Hayley to the left, and then back, and

then forward. It was a good thing the Chalandra was relatively maneuverable because she didn't have frag all for weapons.

"I'm scanning the HaulNet for anything waiting for our signature," Quark said for Hayley's benefit. "Tibs, you have to keep us from getting fragged before I've got confirmation."

"Doing my best, Colonel," Tibor replied. "I told you before; I'm not a very good pilot. I got barely passing marks on-"

"I don't give a shit," Quark replied. "Keep us from getting dead."

"Aye, Colonel. I've got three starships incoming. Looks like Republic Patrollers."

"Planetary Defense?" Quark asked.

"No. Republic Navy."

"No hail?"

"No, sir."

"Frag me. What the hell are they doing? Shoot first and ask questions later? Bastards. Hal, can you kindly ask the digital freak-monkey to scan for anything from Don Pallimo?"

"He doesn't like being called-"

"Just do it."

"Aye, sir. Gant, did Don Pallimo leave us a communique?"

"I've always liked that word," Gant replied. "Scanning."

"They're trying to box us in, Colonel," Tibor said.

"Well, don't fragging let them," Quark snapped.

"I'm doing my best."

Hayley was nearly dragged out of her seat as the Chalandra shuddered, Tibor pushing it harder than it was intended to go.

"Do you remember that part where I said don't get us dead?" Quark said.

"Hold tight, Tibs, the scan is almost complete," Hayley said. "Isn't it?"

"Affirmative, Witchy," Gant replied. "I'm picking up a Crescent Hauler secured beacon about twenty-thousand klicks from here."

"Gant's reading a beacon," Hayley said.

"I don't see any cargo ships out there," Tibor said. "Where is it coming from?"

"Who gives a shit?" Quark said. "HaulNet is top-level security. The Nephies aren't smart enough to break in, not unless they grabbed the real Gant and nobody bothered to mention that, either. Watch your six, damn it!"

The Chalandra shook as something hit the rear. A warning signal sounded from the pilot seat ahead of her.

"Shit," Tibor said. "Sorry."

"I need a new pilot," Quark said.

"I told you-" Tibor started to reply.

"I don't care. Hal, where's the beacon?"

"Gant, pass it into the ship's computer and get the coordinates over to the pilot's station."

"Aye, Witchy. Done."

"I've got it," Tibor said.

"On the other side of the fragging Patrollers," Quark said. "Great. Get us around them."

"Hold on."

The Chalandra shuddered again, and Hayley was pressed back into her seat as Tibor pegged the throttle. She could tell how he was maneuvering from the pressure on her body. Vectoring hard to port, angling up, dipping down, rolling over. The pleasure cruiser had to be somewhat agile, or they would have been dead already.

"Witchy, we're being hailed," Gant said.

"Colonel, someone's hailing us," she said, passing the message on.

"Put it up."

The energy emitted by the projector at the front of the bridge allowed her to view a fuzzy outline of the display, which appeared to be a very calm, uniformed Republic Navy Officer.

"This is Commander Wilson of the Nevada," the man said. "Cut your engines, or you will be destroyed."

"Are you fragging kidding me, Wilson?" Quark snapped back. "You tried to destroy me the second I came out of the disterium field. What's your damn problem, son?"

"We know why you're here," Wilson replied. "And your intent."

"To grab a few beers with an old friend? That ain't illegal, last time I checked."

"You're very amusing, Captain," Wilson said, his tone anything but amused. "You have five seconds to comply."

Hayley glanced back at Quark. His qi was angry, confused, and amused. Neither one of them had any clue what Wilson was talking about, or why the Republic was trying to blow them up.

"Kill the projection," Quark said.

It vanished a moment later.

"Bastards know they can't catch us, so they're hoping we'll stop. Tibs, when I give the word, open the forward hold." Quark stood up. "Get us on top of the package. I'll snatch it, and then we get the frag out of here."

"As long as they don't blow us to shit while you're out there," Tibor said.

"Hal, can you help out with that?"

"I don't have any naniates."

"But the people on the Navy ships probably do, even if they don't know it. Use the Chalandra's array to amplify your signal."

He didn't wait for her to respond, heading off the bridge.

"You and me, Witchy," Tibor said.

The ship rocked again, another near miss.

"Gant, can we hook into the ship's array?"

"Aye, Witchy. One moment. Done."

That was easy.

"Tibor, how far to the beacon?"

"Five thousand and closing fast."

Hayley adjusted her attention, mentally calling out to the naniates. She pushed the order through the Chalandra's comm array, amplified much louder than her visor could manage. If they could hear her, they would arrive shortly.

"Hold on," Tibor said. "I'm hitting the brakes."

She was thrown forward against her restraints as Tibor reversed thrust. The first of the naniates started to arrive, the lightest touch on her flesh the only indication they were there, at least until they gathered in enough numbers to turn her black tattoos blue.

"Tibs, I'm in the hold," Quark said, his voice echoing from the bridge's speakers. "Open her up."

"Aye, sir," Tibor replied.

The ship vibrated slightly as the airlocks in the hold below sealed off the rest of the ship and pumps pushed air back into compressed chambers. It only took a handful of seconds for the process to complete, and then the hydraulics started opening the cargo doors at the bottom of the ship's hold.

Hayley unbuckled herself and stood up. She could feel the collective weight of the naniates across her entire body, clinging to the intricate lines of the tattoos covering her. They were everywhere except where Bale had cut her. She moved to the center of the bridge as the Chalandra slowed to a near-stop.

"I've got visual on the beacon," Quark said. "Standby."

"Witchy, we've got missiles incoming," Tibor said.

"How many?"

"Three."

She sent a new command out to the naniates to move them.

The molecular machines glowed as they burned energy, vanishing from her arms in the millions, splitting up and jumping to the warheads, breaking through the phase of spacetime to make the trip in an instant.

They clung to the projectiles, enough of them expelling energy to alter the vector of the missiles so they swept harmlessly past the ship. The ones that didn't burn themselves out returned to her.

"Shit," Tibor said. "They're switching to plasma."

Hayley cursed under her breath. It was much easier for her to have the naniates move a missile than try to deal with plasma.

She concentrated, sending the command out to the naniates to surround the Chalandra and create a web of energy to act as a shield. They wanted to resist her command. They knew the action was going to destroy them, and they didn't want to be destroyed.

They didn't have a choice.

Whatever it was about their programming, whatever had happened to her when Thraven had given her the Gift and it had nearly killed her, they couldn't refuse her. As long as she pushed them hard enough, they had to do what she asked.

They flared blue around her, and then vanished, moving out into the void. The outside of the Chalandra started to glow with their light as they passed powerful energy across the ships's hull until they were strong enough to vaporize the superheated gas that was headed their way.

"I'm closing on the beacon," Quark said. "Thirty seconds, and then we GTFO."

"Aye, Colonel," Tibor said.

Hayley continued to push the naniates, not giving them an option to retreat. She could feel the strain building against her mind, threatening to wear her out. Thirty seconds. She could manage that long.

"The Republic Patrollers are closing in," Tibor said. "It doesn't matter if we stop their attack if we can't get back out."

"First things first," Quark said. "I've got the package. It's fragging small. Too small for the Republic assholes to pick up. Heading back in."

"Tibor, we don't have time for him to push back," Hayley said. "You need to scoop him up."

"I don't know if I have the skill to-"

"Do it!" she snapped.

"Okay," he replied.

The strain was increasing, the Republic Patrollers continuing to fire on them, hoping to break through her shield. She was calling more of the naniates in, pulling them from the ships that were attacking them. The Navy had no idea they were fueling the defense, and by coming closer, they were making things easier.

She nearly lost her concentration when the Chalandra jerked in space, adjusting vectors.

"What the frag are you doing?" Quark shouted.

"Coming to you, sir," Tibor replied.

"I don't think-"

"Keep going," Hayley interrupted. She gritted her teeth, the mental toll accelerating.

The ship jolted forward.

"Aw, hell," Quark said. "Whooo, I'm in!" he added a moment later. "Get us out of here."

"Witchy, hold on," Tibor said.

Hayley fell backward into the command chair, grabbing

the buckle and strapping herself in right before she was thrown hard to the side and back, the thrusters shaking the ship as Tibor pegged them to full.

"Gant, set coordinates and get us out of here," Hayley said.

"Destination?" Gant replied.

"Anywhere but here."

"I'm unfamiliar-"

"Not funny."

The AI laughed. "Setting coordinates."

Hayley let go of the naniates, the weight falling away from her mind. The colors in her head swirled and spun, fading in and out. She gripped the sides of her seat tightly, fighting to stay conscious, listening to the disterium reactors beginning to whine as they powered up.

"Tibs, get us clear!" Quark shouted.

"Almost there," Tibor replied.

The Chalandra shook, hit by something. The rhythmic sound of the reactors paused, and for a brief second, Hayley thought they weren't going to make it after all.

Then the sound returned, at a higher pitch than before.

It faded as the Chalandra entered FTL.

Hayley slumped back in the chair, lightheaded and exhausted. She remembered to breathe, dragging in and exhaling deep, long breaths.

"That was too close," Tibor said.

"We made it," she replied between gulps of air. "Thanks to you."

"And to you. We would have been dead otherwise."

The door to the bridge slid open. Hayley turned her head as Quark moved beside her. She still couldn't see straight, and his qi was hard to separate from the kaleidoscope exploding in her head.

"Tibor, get out," Quark said.

His voice was harsh. He was pissed.

"Yes, sir," Tibor said.

Hayley could hear him moving past them and off the bridge.

It didn't take a genius to know she was in trouble.

"Colonel, I-" she started to say.

"You want to do this now, or you want to wait until your head is a little clearer?" he asked.

"Now," she replied, moving to stand.

"Stay seated, soldier."

"Yes, sir."

Maybe he loved her like a daughter, but that had never meant she was immune to being chewed out when she did something wrong, and this was no different.

"Who the hell do you think you are?" he shouted, storming across the bridge in front of her. "I give a damned order, you follow it. I give Tibor an order, he follows it. It isn't a hard fragging concept to understand. But now you think you have some right to counter my orders? Is that what you think, Witchy?"

"No, sir," she said quietly.

"What?" he replied, moving in close.

"No, sir!" she snapped back, more strongly.

"I told Tibor to wait for me, not send a hundred ton beast

charging at me, maw gaping open like I'm fragging Jonah. I'm sure you felt the way he was flying. Shit, I think you could do a better job, and you can't even see most of what's out there. What the hell were you thinking telling him to keep at it?"

"I was thinking I wanted us to escape, sir," she said.

"And since when do you have the right to think for yourself during a combat operation?"

"I'm sorry, sir. It was a mistake, sir."

"A mistake?" he screamed, getting down in her face. She didn't flinch. "A mistake is leaving your fly open after you take a piss. A mistake is picking up a hooker on Athena and believing her when she says she's been sterilized and then having to pay fragging child support for the next twenty years. Countering your superior's order is not a fragging mistake. It's willful fragging ignorance. I've been a soldier for almost three hundred years, damn it. Do you know how many lifers make it as long as I have?"

"Almost none, sir."

"Almost none. But suddenly, I'm incapable of making a damned decision?"

"No, sir."

"Damn it, Hal, I need you to set the example. You're all I've got left of the original crew. Hell, you're damn near all I've got left in general." His voice softened considerably. "I know you're trying to look out for me. I know you want to get back at the Nephies for what they did. But you have to respect chain of command. You make me look bad in front of Tibor, that's one thing because I know he's solid. We pick up some greenies, and you make me look bad, that's a level of respect I can never get back. They'll think I'm giving you special treatment, or that I'm soft."

"I know, sir," she replied. She had screwed up. She knew it. "I'm sorry, sir."

"I know you are," he said. His voice had completely

shifted, becoming gentle and tender. "And I know you saved our lives. I could see the plasma headed for my face and the web of naniates that stopped it. I'm not blind. You made the right call, but you made it in the wrong way."

"Yes, sir," she said.

"I'd have you scrub the decks, but this bitch is already squeaky-clean. Give me some time, and I'll think of a suitable punishment."

"Yes, sir."

"In the meantime, give me a damn hug."

She smiled, leaning forward and embracing him.

"Between you and me, I love you, kid," he said.

"I love you, too," she replied.

"How are you feeling?"

"Washed."

"I bet. Where the hell are we going?"

"I don't know. I told Gant to send us anywhere but here."

"No comfort from that. At all."

"What about the package?"

Quark lifted his hand. "It's a projector. When Pallimo said he would leave a message for us, I expected a transmission, not a physical device." He laughed. "Smart though. Too small for PD or the Navy to notice he left out here. He must have known there was trouble brewing."

"What kind of trouble?"

"That's the million coin question, isn't it? I'll bet my ass it has to do with Thetan and the Nephilim. If he knows we made it off Kelvar with the chip, he's going to be running damage control."

"That involves the Republic Navy? How would he manage that?"

"Lots of questions right now, kid. Not a lot of answers. But hopefully, once we talk to Pallimo, we'll have more of a clue." He stood up, backing away from her and tossing the projector onto the floor. "Let's see what the bossman has to say."

The projector turned on. Hayley didn't try to focus enough to see it. She was tired, and she already knew what the Don looked like.

"It's Pallimo," Quark said for her. "Looking pretty good."

"He's not alive."

Quark laughed. "So he always looks good."

"Colonel," Don Pallimo said. "I trust you've retrieved me from the cold emptiness of space. I'm sorry to contact you this way. I'm sure picking me up wasn't a piece of cake."

"What's with the cake references today?" Quark said.

"It seems the Nephilim may have compromised the Haul-Net, which is the reason for this alternate method of communication. I'm not sure how they managed to crack my keys just yet, but my people are looking into it. Anyway, I intercepted a private GalNet transmission regarding your ship. It originated from Kelvar, signed by Evolent Jol."

"That's not possible," Hayley said. "Jol is dead."

"I know, kid," Quark said. "Hold on."

"They knew the ship you were traveling in, and a separate missive was passed on to the Republic through their secured channels claiming you were a rogue actor from the Outworlds intent on crashing a high-yield explosive into Augustine's capital. I'm sure you've already experienced the warm welcome the Republic had waiting for you. I would have warned you ahead of time, but you were already FTL."

Quark laughed again. "An explosive? Terrorists? I can't believe the Republic went for that bullshit."

"If it came through official channels, there's no reason for them not to," Hayley said.

"True. Damn. No wonder they wanted to shoot first and then talk."

"I've redirected my doppelgänger to Athena. I assume that

will be satisfactory, as I understand you're in need of new crew members. It will be there for four days, awaiting your arrival. If you don't show, we'll assume you were killed. Again, Colonel, my sincerest condolences on your losses. You too, Hayley. I'm very sorry, my dear."

Hayley's eyes teared slightly at the comment. Don Pallimo was like a doting grandfather to her, even if he was a neural network pretending to be a living human being.

The projector shut off. Quark didn't move for a few seconds, staring at it.

"I guess that's it, kid," he said, turning back to her.

"How do we know the Don left the projector?" she asked.

"You think it's another trap?"

"Everything has been so far, and I remember a certain someone telling me to always treat everything as a trap. If the Nephilim really have hacked the HaulNet, there's nothing stopping them from creating a projection that looks and sounds like the Don, and leaving it out there for us to find."

"We can't rule it out completely, but it isn't likely. How would Thetan get a ship over to Augustine before us?"

"That depends on where his assets were positioned in the first place, doesn't it? Besides, he had more time than we're allowing. I spent almost a week on the mend on Kelvar, and Bale got away."

"The leftover genetic mutant furball? I forgot about him. You think he made the call out?"

"Using Evolent Jol's keys."

"Damn. I should have sent Tibs out to hunt him down back on Kelvar."

"Do you have to keep calling him Tibs?" Hayley asked. "He doesn't like it."

"For now. Once he earns a better call sign, he'll get a better call sign. Unless you want me to call him 'Shithead?' That's what I usually end up calling pilots."

"I don't think he'd like that any better than Tibs."

"Beggars can't be choosers. You got a thing for the hairless doggie?"

She sighed. "We're friends. He looks out for me. I look out for him."

"Friends with a Nephie. Did you ever think that would happen?"

"Not in a million years."

"Guess you never know what life's going to throw at you."

"I guess not."

"Tell Gant to get us out of FTL and redirect to Athena. Then go get some rest."

"Aye, sir."

"On the floor," he added. "One hour, no more."

"Aye, sir."

Quark picked up the projector, heading for the door to the bridge.

"What are you going to do with that?" Hayley asked.

"Throw it out the fragging airlock. If it is a trap, I'm not waiting for this thing to blow up in my face. We've had enough of that already."

4

ATHENA WAS A FRINGE PLANET, LOCATED ON THE OUTWORLD side of the spread of worlds that separated the two governing factions of the galaxy. It was a well-known planet among mercenaries, a place famous for being a rich recruiting ground for new employees. Any soldier who wanted to join up with a merc unit found their way to the planet eventually, usually spending at least a short stint as a fighter in the Ring.

It was a much better location for the meet with Pallimo than Augustine had been, leading Hayley to believe that maybe the Don had already guessed they would hit trouble on their way into the Republic world, and had adjusted before they even knew the shit they were stepping into. It wouldn't be the first time the Don was a step ahead, but it left her to wonder why he had directed them to Augustine in the first place, knowing there was a chance they wouldn't make it out alive.

Then again, what if the whole thing was a setup? What if Thetan had made the message, dropped the projector, and hedged his bets? If the Republic Navy didn't manage to kill them before they grabbed the package, then he would have a second chance.

The only wrinkle in that line of thinking was that she didn't think Thetan wanted them dead. They still had the data chip containing the Nephilim's research on how to use the naniates to modify the different Extant races like the Goreshin. Honorant Devain had said there was other research taking place in other parts of the galaxy. She had claimed they had made progress with super intellect in addition to super soldiers. Was it that intellect that had cracked the HaulNet's security?

For as much as they had learned and experienced on Kelvar, they still didn't know all that much about what was really going on.

Whatever. The outcome was the same. They had redirected the Chalandra to Athena, earning another day of so-called rest and relaxation before dropping into the planet's orbit thirty-two hours later. Their luck was a little better this time, and they managed to bring the luxury cruiser to ground in the spaceport without incident.

The planet's capital was Minerva. Like most Fringe cities, it was a few dozen years behind on the latest tech and had its fair share of slums and hovels and shitty places where it wasn't safe for most people to go. It also had its share of individuals from a number of planets who had come in search of something else, or to escape from something worse. They crowded the city, either trying to make new lives for themselves in the middle of nowhere, or trying to get picked up as crew for the hundreds of merchants, pirates, mercenaries, and other assorted rabble that did some kind of business on the planet.

It was dark by the time they received final clearance from Athena Control to disembark from the Chalandra. The entire process had been delayed because of the nature of the starship. Pleasure cruisers just didn't go to Athena on purpose, which created a lot of questions Quark was forced to spend hours answering. Questions he didn't want to answer, but he didn't have a choice if they ever wanted to step off the ship.

"Well, that was like having my teeth ripped out with a rusty-ass knife," he said, joining Hayley and Tibor in their makeshift armory. "You'd think they'd know me by now. I've only been to this planet a hundred times, and it's not like there's a glut of individuals with a pretty mug like mine. Idiots."

"They probably just couldn't believe you traded the Quasar for this thing," Hayley said.

"I wouldn't believe that bullshit either. Of course, I had to make up some stupid lie about her being in space dock under repair and renting out this ugly thing to make a quick run over for some fresh meat. The good news is, I didn't get the impression the Nephilim have their hooks into this planet yet. I name-dropped Devain, Jol, Thetan, even Tibs here, and they gave me the old dumb-eyes."

"Do you know where we're supposed to meet Don Pallimo?" Hayley asked.

"Nope. I'm sure he'll make himself known when it's convenient. In the meantime, we'll take a stroll over to Duke's to see if there's any meat worth trying out."

"Trying out?" Tibor said.

"Damn right," Quark said. "You think any old soldier can become a Rider? Most individuals have to pass muster. You got to do trial by fire."

"Lucky me," Tibor said, sarcastically.

"Damn right, lucky you," Quark replied. "You want to be a Rider; you got to go three rounds with me without getting knocked cold. Needless to say, ninety-nine percent of grunts don't make the cut."

"I could have passed that way, too," Tibor said.

"Maybe I'll drag you down to the fitness bay sometime and make you prove that."

Tibor smiled. "If I win, you stop calling me Tibs?"

"You win, I'll let you pick your own call sign."

"Deal."

They descended the ramp onto the spaceport tarmac. They were one of the smaller ships in the midst of a sea of larger vessels, all of which looked at least fifty years old and were armed and armored for expected confrontation. The shiny silver, sleek lines, and weaponless nature of the Chalandra stood out like a pimple on an ass, pristine and pomp enough to be laughable.

Hayley removed her visor as they reached the tarmac, tucking it into the pocket of the long coat she was wearing over her lightsuit. They were in what Quark called civvie-but-ready status, hiding their weapons and armor beneath loose-fitting clothes that would be easy to get out of or work through in a pinch. She hated to lose the gear, but until they could be certain the Nephilim weren't waiting to spring a trap, it was better for her to blend in.

She raised a hood over her head, hiding her face in shadow and covering her red hair. It wasn't a common color to begin with and was even less common this far from Earth.

Quark slipped on a pair of dark glasses and a tight skull-cap, a glow-in-the-dark middle finger printed on the left side. Tibor stood out the least of the three of them as a human, and if he went to his second form, there would be no way for him to hide. He stuck with a standard shirt and pants over a more stretchable body armor he had taken from the lab beneath the warehouse on Kelvar.

There was a transport that weaved around among the ships, picking up crews and dropping them at the station near the port's arrival terminal, but Quark didn't wait for it, walking briskly from the ship after closing up the ramp with a remote access code linked to his Tactical Command Unit. It was clear from his pace he wanted to get away from the Chalandra as quickly as possible, before anyone associated him with the pleasure boat. It was only a matter of time before he was recognized, but he didn't need to be the center of attention already.

The hike to the terminal took about ten minutes, leaving them standing near a few groups of other travelers all on their way downtown. Each kept to their own, most talking quietly and keeping their business to themselves. One of the groups appeared to be composed of mercenary soldiers on shore leave, and they carried on with the lack of awareness of their surroundings that came from too much time cooped up on a small ship together. They joked and shoved at one another, whooping and cursing and acting like assholes. It was all in good fun and easy to ignore, at least until one them was shoved back into Hayley.

She hadn't been paying attention to them, and the sudden force knocked her back a step. She caught herself easily, turning to face her supposed attacker.

"Excuse me," the man said. His qi was a yellowish pink. Intoxicated.

"Watch your damn step," Quark snapped, moving protectively in front of her as if she needed protection.

"Sorry, grandma," the man replied. "It was an accident. Don't get your panties in a bunch."

Hayley tried to grab Quark's arm before he could react, but even knowing it was coming, she was too slow. He lashed out, taking the cuff of the man's coat, pulling it together and winding it so he could choke the merc and pull him in close.

"What the frag did you call me, boy?" he asked.

The rest of the mercenary's group reacted, moving to

defend their own. Tibor stepped toward them, but Hayley put her hand out to block him.

"He'll take care of it," she said. "There are only six of them."

Tibor laughed.

"Why don't you let him go, grandma?" one of the other mercs said. "We don't want trouble."

"You don't want trouble?" Quark said. "One of you calls me grandma again, you all go back to your XO with broken noses."

"You gonna fight us all by yourself?" a third mercenary asked, pausing dramatically before he uttered the final word. "Grandma."

Quark smiled. Then he used his free hand to take off his glasses.

Hayley enjoyed watching the merc's qi turn stark white when he realized who he had been fragging with. Quark's reputation was what had drawn Thetan's attention in the first place. He wanted to try his Goreshin against the best. Too bad for him, his best hadn't been up to the task.

"Uh. Shit. Colonel Quark. I. Uh. I didn't know it was you."

Quark let him go. It was unlike him. "Lucky for you, I'm not here to beat the shit out of idiots," he said. "I'm looking for some new Riders. You assholes know if there's anyone decent on your roster?"

There was an unwritten rule among mercenaries that you didn't poach talent from one another. Quark's Riders were the exception to that rule and all of the others. He did what he wanted because he had earned it.

"No, sir," the first idiot said. "We're not at your level, sir."

"What about a pilot?"

The man didn't answer right away.

"You have a decent pilot?" Quark asked.

"I can't, sir. Captain Torrl will kill me."

"I'll kill you if you don't."

"We do, sir, but she's not available."

"Why the frag not?"

"She's incapacitated at the moment."

"How exactly do you mean that?" Quark said, raising his eyebrow.

One of the other mercenaries picked up the slack. "She went to Duke's, sir. Got slackered, came back to the ship to sleep it off. She'll be out another four to six hours at least."

"A pilot that drinks herself to oblivion?" Quark said. "I like it. She human?"

"Trover, sir."

"A female Trover pilot? I've never heard of it."

"She's special, sir. That's why Captain will kill me if you take her."

"To be honest, I don't give a shit if he kills you or not. My interest is piqued. Witchy, let's make sure we make a stop on our way back. Which one of these buckets is yours?"

"Sir," the mercenary said, not very eager to be the reason their company lost their pilot.

"I promised I would break your nose and the noses of all your friends. You give me the intel; I leave you able to breathe normally."

"The Gunner," he said. "You can look her up on the board." He pointed toward a display on the wall.

The transport to the city proper glided to a stop beside them. Quark slipped his glasses back on as the doors to it slid open.

"Have a nice day," he said, stepping inside.

The mercenaries watched him, remaining in the station, deciding to take the next shuttle in.

"A Trover female?" Hayley said. "I didn't think they ever left Tro."

"She must be something else," Quark said. "What are the

29

odds we might land a pilot on our first try? I'm starting to get a good feeling about our trip here."

"I hope you're right, Colonel. I'm already getting tired of things going to hell everywhere we go."

It would have been nice to leave it at that. To take a quiet shuttle ride from the spaceport into downtown Minerva.

That was their plan, but somebody, somewhere, had other plans.

Something in the city exploded.

5

"WHAT THE FRAG?" QUARK SAID.

Hayley was white-blinded as the heat energy from the sudden fireball erupted across her vision, pushing out the color of the qi surrounding her on the transport. It came from somewhere downtown, a massive and sudden flare a few kilometers away.

The explosion had started to fade when the sound and the shockwave hit, a hard roar that hurt her ears along with a shudder in the ground that rattled the shuttle. The vehicle came to a sudden stop, all of its riders looking and murmuring comments to one another.

"Fragging war zone," someone said.

"Hope that wasn't Duke's," someone else commented.

"Your attention, please," the shuttle driver said over the comm. "Your attention, please. We've been ordered to return all passengers to the spaceport. I repeat, all passengers are ordered to return to the spaceport."

"You have to be kidding me," Quark said, looking over at her and Tibor. "Coincidence?"

He froze in place. Hayley knew the look. He was either looking at something nobody else could see, or he was getting a message through his TCU, which was hooked into his mechanical eyes.

"Shit," he said. "No rest for the wicked, and that means us."

"What's up?" Hayley asked.

"Don Pallimo just passed me a message. Seems I might have been wrong about the Nephilim's presence here."

"How would Thetan know we were here?" Hayley asked. "Pallimo passed us the location on a physical device."

"Could be they're tracking Pallimo, then," Quark said. "Hoping he'll lead them to us."

"That still doesn't work," Hayley countered. "Why attack before we get there?"

Quark froze again and then started to laugh. "Oh, this is fragging rich, Witchy. It appears the Nephies just snatched the Don. They don't know we're here yet. They're grabbing him to trade for the data chip when we arrive."

Hayley couldn't help but smile with him. Because these Nephilim didn't know the truth about Don Pallimo. All of them that ever had were dead.

They thought they had hacked into the Crescent Hauler's network, and followed the transmissions to determine the Don's whereabouts. They thought he was meeting the Riders on Athena, and what better way to get what they wanted than to capture one of the most powerful men in the galaxy?

The joke was on them. The Nephies hadn't captured who they thought they had. They also didn't know he was able to transmit silently to Quark.

"Pallimo did this on purpose, didn't he?" Hayley asked.

"Put these assholes right where we want them?" Quark replied. "I wouldn't bet against it. He knows how bad we want to get a handle on Thetan. This may be our chance."

"First, we have to get downtown," Tibor said.

The shuttle was turning around, while emergency vehicles were racing past above it.

"Those assholes killed more innocent people," Hayley said.

"Not too many innocents on Athena, but sure," Quark replied. "We need to stop this thing."

"On it," Hayley said.

She started forward, moving down the aisle past the other passengers. There were three cars on the shuttle, separated by a narrow gap. She hopped the first, rushing through toward the front.

She watched the qi of the other passengers as she moved. Most of it was red and blue, the mercenaries calm but slightly pissed about having to go back to their ships. A few were yellow with drunkenness. A couple had tinges of purple. Almost all of the humans on the transport were carrying naniates to one degree or another. Infected, so to speak, though they probably had no idea.

She froze when she recognized the red-gold tinge of the Gift in one of them. The individual was sitting, facing away from her, looking out of the car. A man with longer hair and a light frame, he seemed to feel her vision on him because he turned their his at the same time she noticed him.

Red qi flowed from the passenger, along with red-gold naniates. He lashed out toward her, attempting to shove her back.

The naniates came close before freezing, stopping in place and refusing to make contact. Hayley reached under her coat for her gun.

He stood up, surprised by her immunity to the Gift. She thought he would match her, reaching for a weapon of some kind.

He didn't.

He ran.

She raised her gun, but she didn't shoot. She wasn't going to attack someone running away from her, even if they were Nephilim. She lowered the weapon again, grabbing her visor and pulling it over her head to snap it into place.

"Colonel, I've got a positive ID on a Gifted," she said. "He was sitting in the second car, and now he's making a run for it."

"A run where?"

The Gifted opened the doors between the second car and the first. He paused in between, and then jumped off the shuttle, using his Gift to land smoothly.

"He just disembarked. Should I chase him?"

"Negative. We need to stop the transport and get down-town. I'm working the passengers."

Whatever that meant.

She looked back at the Nephilim as the transport went past him. She could swear he waved at her before she turned her head back and charged to the front of the shuttle.

She reached the driver. "Stop the shuttle," she said, before realizing the driver was a bot.

"My apologies, ma'am," it said. "My orders are to return all passengers to the spaceport until further notice."

"I don't care about your orders," she said. "I need to get downtown."

"My apologies, ma'am," it said. "My orders are to return all passengers to the spaceport until further notice."

Hayley sighed. There was never any way to reason with a bot. She reached out for her Meijo, pulling the naniates in from the passengers on the shuttle. They came to rest on her tattoos, and she put her hand on the bot's head.

"Ma'am, it is illegal under Athena Governance Statute ten dot one dot three dot fifteen to make physical contact with any non-organic government employee. Please-"

She sent the naniates into the bot, shorting it out. Sparks flew out from its neck, and then it fell dark in front of her, no longer drawing energy.

The shuttle lurched, its driver no longer monitoring it. She cursed, grabbing the bot and shoving it away. It crashed onto its side on the floor beside her.

She took its place. There was no seat, and the controls were made for a machine, in the form of simple sticks. She took hold of them, trying to manipulate them to get the shuttle going back the other way.

The slightest motion led to a massive adjustment, and she sent the vehicle into too tight of a turn, causing it to slip on its lifting coils. Momentum threw her into the side, and she could hear the other passengers shout as they were knocked around too.

"Witchy, what the frag?" Quark said over the comm. "That's what I get for sending a blind girl to drive a bus."

"The controls are touchy," she replied. "There's plenty of qi around; I can see just fine."

"Can you stop this thing?"

"Standby."

She didn't know how to stop it. The sticks were the only controls. She tried pulling them up, thinking it might activate the braking system. The shuttle accelerated, hard enough to send the passengers tumbling backward.

"Damn it, Witchy," Quark said. "You're going to kill us before we get there."

"Sorry," she said, pushing the sticks down. The transport came to a too-abrupt stop, throwing everybody forward. "Shit. Sorry."

"Thank all that is righteous we stopped moving," Quark said through the comm. His voice cut through the air a moment later. "Alright meat. Change in plans. My name's Colonel Quark. You may have heard of me. I've got business downtown, and that's where this shuttle's headed. I'm looking for some fresh meat, so if you're looking to upgrade your career, and you want to impress me, hang with. Otherwise, get the frag off."

Hayley looked back, watching most of the mercenaries head for the exits. They weren't afraid of whatever Quark wanted the shuttle for. From their qi, it seemed they knew they didn't measure up to the Riders' standards, proving the Colonel's reputation was a double-edged sword.

One individual did remain. A big, furry Curlatin. He looked like an oversized teddy bear with massive black oval eyes. He was looking back at her, and he flashed her a smile and a thumbs up. His qi was a bright yellow and blue. He was excited.

"What's your name?" she asked.

"Narrl," he replied. His voice was a low rumble. "Yours?"

"Witchdoctor," she replied. "Witchy for short."

"Pleasure."

Hayley nodded. Quark and Tibor came through the linking hatch, with two other mercs in tow. Both were human. One was an obvious Outworlder. The other carried herself like a former Republic soldier.

"A Curlatin?" Quark said. "Nice. Name's Quark."

"Narrl."

"This here is Lana and Kavil. You'll excuse me if I don't make small talk, but you need to live long enough for it to be worth my time. Witchy, I'm subbing you out for Tibs at the controls."

"Roger," she said.

Tibor squeezed her shoulder on her way past him.

"We'd better get moving," Hayley said. "It sounds like PD is headed our way."

6

"Ah, Planetary Defense," Quark said. "You can always count on them to frag up the wrong damn side every single time." He raised his voice. "Tibs, let's go."

"Better hold on," Hayley said. "The controls are-"

The shuttle accelerated forward, and then into a tight turn. Hayley braced herself between the floor and the ceiling, holding on while they whipped around.

"Sensitive," she finished.

"Maybe I should have let you drive," Quark said.

The whooping of PDs sirens was audible to the rest of them now. Hayley leaned over to look back out the window, able to see the heated contrails of the defense drones closing in from above.

"What do you want to do about those?" Hayley asked.

Quark reached under his coat, pulling his pistol. He turned it over and held it out toward the two human mercenaries.

"First test," he said. "Take out the drones."

They scrambled for the gun. Lana grabbed it first and

then moved to one of the windows. She kicked at it, hitting it three times before it fell away and into the street. Then she leaned out.

Narrl grumbled something, watching the action.

"Sorry," Quark said. "I don't have a gun that'll fit in your hand."

The Curlatin laughed. "No problem, Colonel." He stood up, producing a gun of his own. "I've got you covered."

He had to duck to move down the aisle, going to one of the exits. He grabbed it, forcing it open with brute strength, and then vanished from the cab. Hayley could hear his feet on the top of the shuttle.

"We having fun yet, Witchy?" Quark asked.

"Ask me again after we catch up to the Nephilim, sir," she replied.

Tibor had managed to get them turned around, the shuttle heading downtown once more. Lana started shooting from her position out the window, and Narrl fired a shot from his perch on top of the vehicle, his large hand cannon thumping hard. Hayley saw the thrusters of one of the drones die and heard it crash into the ground a few seconds later.

"That one's mine!" Lana shouted.

"No way," Narrl said. "My hit. My kill."

"Bullshit."

Hayley glanced back at Quark. He was loving this. While it felt good to see him happy, she wasn't ready to forget they had been tricked before. She wasn't ready to accept they weren't steering straight into yet another trap.

The Colonel must have had the same thought, because his qi shifted, becoming more serious.

"They're moving Pallimo," he said to her. "Taking him away from downtown to a more secluded location."

"The kind that's easy to launch an ambush from?" she asked.

"My thought, exactly. We need to play this more careful than Kelvar."

"Yes, sir."

Narrl's gun fired again, another roaring round that hit a second drone as it was closing in.

"I think we might have a winner up there," Quark said.

"What should I do, sir?" Kavil asked.

"Stand there and look stupid, meat," Quark replied. "You should have been quicker to grab the gun."

The shuttle was closing in on downtown, reaching cracked and dirty streets surrounded by equally disheveled buildings. Athena hadn't always been a dark Fringe world. It hadn't always been named Athena. Some of the worst skirmishes in the many-years war between the Republic and the Outworlds had taken place here, diminishing it until it was abandoned by most good citizens and replaced with the current consortium. There were always holdovers, and they lived in the tall apartments surrounding the outskirts of the city, holed up there and looking down on the action with a sense of resignation.

There were more drones approaching, greater numbers of them sent to deal with the wayward shuttle and the mercenaries that had the gall to fire back at them. Hayley could hear them buzzing around the shuttle, her visor helping her position the machines to their left and right, judging the distance by the pitch of their thrusters.

"Permission to go up there with Narrl?" she said.

"Granted," Quark replied. "Be careful."

"Roger."

She ran to the hatch Narrl had opened, grabbing the top and swinging herself up and around. The Curlatin glanced at her as she joined him, pulling her pistol.

"I like the headgear," he said. "Good for protecting your eyes."

"Something like that," she replied.

She aimed toward one of the buildings, listening for the drone. It came around the corner and she fired, hitting it square ahead of the thrusters and bringing it down.

"Hrm," Narrl grumbled. "Good shot. You're already with the Colonel, though. Why not give us a chance?"

"Don't worry," she said. "You'll have your chance. Get down!"

She dropped prone on the top of the shuttle as a drone cut across an intersection, opening fire on them. Plasma bolts rained down, slamming the metal around them and melting right through.

Hayley rolled over to check on Narrl. He was laughing.

"I wasn't expecting this when I came down here. I thought maybe I'd find a job with the Panthers or the Crushers. I heard they were looking for new grunts, and my last unit disbanded." He stood up, turning and aiming. His shot nailed the drone that had just flashed past. He looked back at her. "I'm going to make the cut. Fragging Riders. I can't believe my luck."

She tracked another drone across the sky, diving toward Narrl and grabbing his arm to pull him back down.

He didn't budge, too heavy to move. He saw the drone, and he aimed and fired, hitting it square with a large slug. It exploded in mid-air.

He fell to his knees. He had been two seconds too slow, the drone hitting him first. Hayley could smell the burned fur, and see the smoke of the burn drifting up from where the plasma hit him.

He looked at her, confused.

"Shit," he said.

"Today really is your lucky day," she replied. She pushed

him onto his back, leaning over him and reaching to his wound.

"What are you doing?" he asked.

"I'm a doctor," she replied. "A witchdoctor."

She put her hand on the wound as her tattoos started to glow. The Meijo moved down to her hands and into the wound, the naniates pulling the big soldier back together.

She scanned the sky as she worked her magic, watching for more incoming drones. Lana was still shooting at them from the window, and the transport was slowing down.

"Witchy, it's getting too hot out here to keep the ride," Quark said. "We're abandoning ship. Pallimo's got a beacon going."

"Roger," Hayley replied. She pulled her hand away from Narrl's chest. The skin had healed, but it would take some time for his fur to grow back. "All better."

He felt the area, shocked and surprised. "Wow."

"We're on the move, let's go."

The shuttle came to a quick stop, and she jumped off the roof to the ground. Narrl joined her there a moment later, Quark and the others a couple of seconds after that. Quark pointed down an alley, leading them away as the drones passed over the shuttle.

"Where are we?" Tibor asked.

"Minerva," Kavil replied.

"No, I mean, where in Minerva?"

"Shut it, all of you," Quark said. "We're a few blocks from Duke's." He pointed to where most of the smoke was originating. "Looks like the Nephies blew it up after all. Probably trying to keep us from reloading. Bastards."

"Duke's? Gone?" Lana sounded like her heart had been broken.

"Tell me about it," Quark replied. "Keep it moving, PD isn't about to let us wander around the city."

He led them through the alleys and streets perpendicular to the carnage. They were all soldiers, and they all understood his hand signals well enough to stay in a reasonable formation.

The drones continued to criss-cross the streets, while PD patrollers moved closer to the ground, steering anyone still outside to somewhere else. The attack had put the city in lockdown, and soon enough the Governance would start grabbing the same mercenaries that had denied Quark's offer to join them in their hunt of the Nephilim to hunt the Riders instead.

If they were smart, they would get off the planet while they still could.

If PD would let them.

7

"THEY STOPPED," QUARK SAID, TURNING HIS HEAD TO LOOK AT the mercenaries behind him. "Let's give it a few minutes, see if they get underway again." He froze, looking at something behind his eyes. "Pallimo thinks they're done moving. They're tying him up."

Hayley shuddered at the statement. She remembered being tied to a chair. There was nothing good about that memory.

"Did you say Pallimo?" Kavil said. "Like, the Don of the Crescent Haulers Pallimo?"

"Yeah. So?"

"He's here? On Athena?"

"Yeah. So? I told you I had business."

"But. Don Pallimo? You didn't say you had business with Don Pallimo."

"What the frag all does that have to do with anything? We've got work to do, we do it, and we get paid. That's how this whole merc thing works. Or did you just take off your diapie this morning?"

Kavil's face started to flush. Lana and Narrl laughed.

"Where is he?" Hayley asked.

"About two klicks south of here."

Hayley looked out past the edge of the building they were crouched along. PD had stepped up their efforts to locate them, adding ground-based drones and foot soldiers to the hunt. Gant had tapped into their secured channel and had informed her they were under the mistaken impression that Quark had destroyed Duke's.

"Why the frag would I do that?" he had said when she told him. "That's the dumbest thing I've ever heard. I needed that place."

It didn't matter. They wanted him and Hayley and Tibor for questioning. The truth would work itself out later. Or not. They would have someone to blame, regardless.

"We'll need a diversion," Quark said. "Give the PD something to run after. Kavil, Lana, you think you can handle it?"

"Yes, sir," Lana said.

"Yes, sir," Kavil said, again a little behind, and less enthusiastically.

"That's the spirit. Head across that way, make sure they see you. Shoot at them but don't kill anybody. We don't need that shit. Just keep them on you."

"Roger," Lana said. "Where should we meet you?"

"Back at the spaceport. The ship is the Chalandra. You can look her up on the board."

"Yes, sir."

"Now get lost."

The two mercenaries saluted and then headed out into the street together. They were halfway across when PD noticed them, one of the wheeled drones turning and blaring a siren, which drew the attention of the organic enforcement. They shouted and chased after the pair, who sent a few wild shots back at them before disappearing down the alley.

"Lana's impressing me so far," Quark said. "Kavil, not so much."

"How am I doing?" Narrl asked.

"You got shot. We like to not get shot."

"Sorry, sir."

"Don't cry, Gnarley. It's only one part of your grade, and I have a feeling you're still going to impress."

"Yes, sir."

They moved down the street, behind the forces giving chase to Kavil and Lana. They were careful not to make too much noise or move too violently and wind up on the drones' sensors. They managed to cross a few blocks before turning down another alley and being forced to hide for a few minutes while another drone moved through.

"Is Pallimo still static?" Hayley asked.

"Affirmative," Quark replied.

"Did he pass any indication of what we're up against?" Tibor said.

"Sounds like the Nephies hired some mercs for this soiree. From Duke's. Before they blew it up. The defense is a random assortment of meat, plus he thinks the mastermind is an Evolent."

"A what?" Narrl asked.

"You ever seen magic before?" Quark asked.

"No, sir. Not before Witchdoctor started glowing and healed my wound in fifteen seconds flat."

"You're going to see more. Don't be too impressed, though; it's not as cool as it looks."

"Uh. Okay, sir."

"And Witchy here? She hates magic."

"Only that kind of magic," Hayley replied. "I'm a healer. The Nephilim are destroyers. Their naniates feed on anger and hate and blood."

"Whatever you say," Narrl replied. "As long as I get the job, just tell me what to shoot."

"Good man-bear," Quark said. "I like your spirit."

They kept moving, slipping down alleys and hiding when needed, spending another thirty minutes covering the distance to the Don's position. They reached the corner of another run-down structure, and Quark pointed.

"In there," he said.

The building in question was a factory or a garage of some kind. Ten stories tall and beat to hell by the fighting that had gone on around it over the last century. It had two large, roll-up doors at the front, and no windows to speak of.

Hayley could imagine what the inside looked like. Machinery, catwalks, and all kinds of places to hide and jump someone. Everything about this deal was screaming 'trap.'

"I don't like it, Colonel," she said, voicing her reservation.

"Me neither," he replied. "Like I said, we play it smart. There's just as much chance the Nephilim set us up as there is Pallimo set them up, and I'm not in the mood to be captured again."

"So what do we do?" Tibor asked.

"Witchy, how do you feel about running a little recon?" Quark asked.

Hayley smiled. "What do you have in mind?"

8

It was easy for Hayley to break simple locks with the Meijo, especially when they were fashioned with mechanical tumblers instead of electro-magnetics or other digital mechanisms. The apartment building was secured by the mechanical kind, and it was almost zero effort for her to disengage the deadbolt to enter the rear stairwell, climb the stairs to the rooftop, and get a good view of the target from across the street.

It wasn't all that different from her last experience on a rooftop. A building. A captured ally. A Gifted waiting to challenge them.

Hopefully, they could do without the damn Goreshin or the Executioners this time.

She crouched at the edge of the building, looking across and down at the rooftop of the factory. There were no guards she could see, and the distance would be easy to cover, even without her anti-gravity pack.

"Colonel, I'm in position," she said. "Rooftop is clear."

"Roger," Quark replied. "Proceed at your own discretion. Send word when you've got something tasty."

"Roger."

She took a few steps back, getting ready to pounce forward and make the jump. Her lightsuit would handle the impact, as long as she tucked right.

She paused as a form appeared at the corner of her vision. She shifted her head, bringing it into frame.

"What the hell?" she mouthed, identifying the man standing on another rooftop east of her position.

He was small in the distance, but she would have known him anyway. The red-gold of his Gift was hard for her to miss.

He stood there, motionless, for a few seconds. Then he started to run.

She watched him hit where she guessed the corner of his building was, and then fly through the air on golden wings of naniates, covering a hundred meters and heading directly for the top of the factory.

Shit.

If he had seen her, he was going to blow the whole damn rescue operation. But had he seen her?

She couldn't risk it.

She rushed forward, feet tapping the synthcrete until she hit the very edge of the apartment. She bounced off, the augmented musculature in the lightsuit carrying her further than her body could on its own. She was on a collision course with the Nephilim, set to hit the rooftop only seconds behind him.

He hit the roof ahead of her, landing smoothly on his feet and turning in her direction. Then she lost sight of him as she tucked her shoulder, turning and hitting the flat surface in a smooth shoulder-roll. She bounced back to her feet, grabbing her Uin as she came up and flicking it open.

He was gone.

"What the?" she said again, spinning quickly, searching for his qi. "Colonel, the Nephie from the shuttle is here. Somewhere. I think he saw me."

"Shit," Quark said. "Can you grab him before he gets inside?"

Grab him? She couldn't even find him.

She heard footsteps then, moving fast and away from her.

"I'll do my best, sir," she said. Then she joined the chase.

The factory's rooftop was covered with ventilation pipes and both heating and cooling units, as well as water storage, solar arrays, comm arrays, and other assorted crap that made most of the surface less even than where she had landed. There were channels between all of the gear, and she was sure the Gifted was using them, based on the sound of his feet along the ground.

Hayley sprinted after him, moving as quickly as she could. Whoever he was, he was trouble.

She crossed through one of the channels, jumping onto the top of an HVAC unit and looking across the rooftop. She caught sight of his qi a dozen meters ahead, rushing toward the stairwell leading into the building. She cursed, knowing she couldn't afford to let him make it. She bounced forward, taking three quick hops in the lightsuit and then lunging ahead, going airborne toward the door in an effort to cut him off.

He came out of hiding a moment later. Not running toward the door. Leaping in the air, vectoring toward her. He had something in his hand.

She twisted, getting her Uin out in front of her as the weapon he was holding lashed out and struck it. Sparks flew from the device, a web of energy running along the rhodrinium surface. She cut her leap short, coming down in one of the channels, bouncing off the side of an exhaust vent and spinning, kicking out with her foot as he came down beside her.

The strike hit him in the shoulder, bouncing him off the same vent. She followed it up with a quick strike from the Uin, but he ducked under it, throwing his weapon at her.

She wasn't expecting him to let go of it. The stick hit her in the chest, a flash of light bursting from it as it unleashed its paralyzing energy. She dropped to her knees, suddenly unable to move her arms and struggling to breathe.

He walked over to her. She looked up at him, trying to find enough air to tell Quark she was in trouble. He stood there for a moment, looking down at her as if he was trying to decide how he wanted to end her life.

Then he bent over and picked up his nerve stick. He picked up her Uin, too. He turned it over in his hand, examining it. His qi shifted colors. Amusement. Curiosity. There was no anger in it. No malice.

"I don't know who you are," he said. "Or why you're here. Maybe you have business inside. So do I. Take your Uin and go. There's nothing but death waiting through that door."

Then he dropped her blade, turned, and walked away.

She remained there, struggling to keep enough breathe to stay conscious. She heard the door open, and his footsteps fade as he entered.

Who the hell was this guy? He knew enough about the Uin to call it by name. He had disabled her in seconds. His Gift was strong enough he could be a powerful Venerant.

But he was going in there to fight? She knew the Prophets in the Extant were always warring with one another. Was he Thetan's competition, looking to stick it to the so-called Disciple of Thraven?

She fought to get her body to move again, throwing herself against the wall and sliding back to her feet without using her arms.

Nothing but death waiting inside?

Frag that. Robotic doppelganger or not, they still needed Pallimo.

She struggled to get the feeling back in her arms and head and mouth. If she could use the Meijo on herself, she would already be back in business. Instead, it took another three minutes before she was at least able to pick up the Uin and get a little bit of her breath back.

"Colonel," she said softly. "I don't know what's going on, but the Gifted isn't an enemy."

"Roger. You mean he's on our side?"

"I wouldn't say that. I don't know. He caught me on the roof. He could have killed me, but he didn't."

"Shit. Lucky for him. Abort the recon; we'll make our move on the front door."

"Sir," Hayley said, remembering their one-sided conversation on the Chalandra's bridge. "I'd like to continue the mission."

"Witchy, we don't know what the deal is in there. We don't know frag all about this guy, except he put you to ground, and I know that ain't easy."

"Understood, sir," she replied. "But I don't trust any of this. I'm a little stunned, but unharmed. I can complete the mission."

She was already walking toward the doorway while she spoke. She wasn't going to outright defy him again, but hopefully, she wouldn't have to retreat.

"If I were any other Rider, you would let me continue, Colonel," she said when he hesitated. "And you know it."

She could almost feel the heat of his fear and frustration. She had never given him much of a choice about becoming a soldier. The only decision he had been able to make was whether to keep her close or watch her go off and fight somewhere else, for someone else.

51

"Continue the mission," he said. "We'll be standing by."

"Yes, sir," she replied.

She reached the now open door and started descending, careful to stay quiet. She didn't know what the Gifted was doing, or what she was walking into, but she couldn't afford to be caught half-crippled. She took the stairwell down, bypassing the administrative offices at the top levels.

She was on the third floor when she came across the first body.

She couldn't tell that much about him, not when his qi was already gone. She knew he was dead, and she hadn't heard a gunshot. She also didn't see any sign of naniate-infused blood. Had the Gifted killed him with his naniates, or with the shock stick? The weapons were intended to disable, but they could be adjusted to make them fatal.

She went down another two floors, reaching the ground level. The stairwell led out into a small corridor. There were two more mercenaries already down here, also bloodlessly murdered.

She shook her arms as she walked down the hallway, the feeling finally beginning to return. The pins and needles were painful but better than being paralyzed.

She moved carefully to the corner, peeking out around it. Another guard was on the ground. The Gifted was up ahead, nearing a heavier door that probably led out to the factory floor.

His naniates flared as he pushed through the door, the red-gold energy bright in her vision.

A moment later, the screaming began.

9

She ran down the corridor, rushing to the door as shouts and screams and gunfire echoed from the factory floor.

"Colonel, the Gifted is on the floor. He's attacking the Nephilim."

"Roger. Do you have eyes on Pallimo?"

"Negative."

"Get the door for us, will you?"

"Roger."

She moved through the heavy door. There were two dead mercenaries at her feet. This time they were bleeding, their throats cut by an edged weapon. A Uin? She looked down at the aisle between two heavy pipes. The Gifted was in front of her, hand up and naniates flowing from it. A mercenary was thrown aside, slamming hard into the pipe with a loud clang. Bullets hung in the air in front of the man, stopped from making contact.

She wanted to follow him, to tail him and grab Pallimo as soon as she located him. Those weren't the orders. She broke to the left, along a metal-grated floor over some kind of dark slurry. She could see the tops of the large roll-up doors from her position. It was her job to open them.

She ran along the grating, her feet making a lot of noise. She wasn't surprised when a merc rotated out in front of her, rifle already up and poised to fire. She skipped sideways as the first bullets whipped past where she should have been, using her feet to spring off the pipe beside her. She flicked open her Uin, convincing her arms to work as she brought the weapon down on the target's weapon, slicing through the muzzle. She reversed herself, throwing a hard punch into the side of his head that dropped him to the floor.

The move brought her in line with the intersection. There was another group of mercenaries there, and they shouted at her appearance, rushing and shooting.

But she was already through and on the other side, sprinting for the door. Why fight them all herself when she didn't have to?

She turned the corner, rushing down the side of some other massive machine and along the wall. She could see where the equipment ended and the open floor space for the delivery vehicles began. As she neared it, a body went flying past her and slammed into the wall.

"Colonel, I'm at the door," she said, reaching the locking mechanism on the roll-up.

She crouched beside it, looking out toward the center of the room.

Don Pallimo was suspended in mid-air, bound and gagged and held by the Gift. The Gifted was at the back of the room, surrounded by mercs, moving like a blur as he fought them. There were more mercenaries on the catwalks above the area, rushing into position and preparing to shoot down at them both.

She kicked the lock on the door, snapping it and sending

the metal barrier spinning back up into its cradle. Quark and the others were waiting right behind it, and they stormed into the factory, taking quick inventory of the situation.

Tibor shifted and grew as his body morphed into its second form, his overclothes tearing and his armor stretching over his mass. He bunched himself and sprang upward, powerful legs carrying him to the lowest of the catwalks and the mercs stationed there. He tore into them, grabbing them with large claws and throwing them off the platform to the ground.

Quark took aim at some of the more distant shooters, the combination of his mechanical eyes and sidearm more than adequate to knock out the targets.

Narrl laughed as he started shooting into the group the Gifted was buried within, knocking them down one by one.

Don Pallimo looked down from his invisible prison, watching the entire scene unfold with blank interest. He wasn't alive, so he had no qi. Just a flow of energy that revealed an outline of his form to her.

Narrl and Quark moved laterally, angling toward cover as the initial surprise of their attack began to wane, and the mercenaries got under cover of their own, beginning to regroup. Tibor leaped from one catwalk to the next, taking hits from the soldiers closest to him, his body sprouting bursts of purple that slowly started to fade.

The Gifted dropped the last of his opponents, turning toward Hayley. Still, his qi didn't shift to angry red. Instead, he seemed almost satisfied she hadn't followed his instructions.

She discovered why a few seconds later.

They came from outside, closing in from the rear, through the same door she had just opened. Nephilim Servants, their silver qi flat as they started shooting. The Evolent was at the rear of their line, filled with red and gold.

Hayley barely managed to get out of the way, bouncing sideways and into a more narrow chasm between machines. Bullets pounded the corner of the metal, skipping off and ricocheting away.

Quark and Narrl turned on them, firing into the masses. Narrl probably had no idea his rounds wouldn't kill the Servants, but Quark knew better. He aimed for their hands and legs, taking away their offensive capability or making it harder for them to stand.

The Servants moved further into the factory, firing back at the pair and forcing them to retreat.

"Damn trap," Quark said over the comm. "They've got Pallimo, but Pallimo thinks he's got them, when they've really got us all. Bastards."

"What do we do, sir?" Hayley asked.

"We still need to grab Pallimo. This is a battle, not the whole damn war."

"Roger. We need to take out the Evolent to get him loose."

"Too many fragging Servants. I-"

He stopped talking. Hayley watched as the Gifted man charged into the mass of Nephilim soldiers, a pair of Uin flashing as he started removing heads, his naniates coursing through him, increasing his strength and speed.

"Tibs, help him out," Quark said.

"Roger," Tibor replied.

Then the Goreshin was dropping from the catwalks above, slamming one of the Servants to the ground and viciously ripping his claws through its neck. He growled as he lunged into another, lifting it and throwing it into a few more to knock them off-balance.

The Servants continued firing, but the Gifted was catching their rounds and redirecting them back into the shooter. The slugs made dents in the soldiers, but not enough to keep them out of the fight.

It was all enough to get the Evolent involved. She leaped forward on her Gift, launching her attack on the other Gifted. He broke off his fight with the Servants, turning to face her and throwing his Gift out.

She raised her hands, blocking it, pushing back with her naniates. Trillions of molecular machines hovered in the air between the two of them, thick enough they became almost visible as a sheen on the air.

Hayley made her move, rushing from cover toward the Gifted and the shooter. They were intent on one another and didn't see her coming.

The Servants did. They adjusted their aim, ready to fire. Tibor crashed into them, throwing them aside, knocking them down, and clearing Hayley's path to the Evolent.

The Evolent saw her coming. She tried to reach out with her other hand, to attack her with the Gift and still defend against her opponent. She wasn't strong enough to do both. The Gifted man's naniates blasted into her, throwing her hard to the ground and choking her. She lost control over Don Pallimo's prison, and he dropped to the floor, rolling onto his back.

Narrl crossed from the corner, charging toward the bound man, shooting at the Servants as he did. He scooped him up in one massive hand, throwing him over his furry shoulder and changing direction.

Hayley neared the Evolent and the Gifted man. The Evolent was struggling to stay in the fight, and she threw back a blast of her Gift that managed to break the man's defenses. He was thrown backward into a group of Servants, forced to fight them to protect himself.

Hayley reached the other woman, jumping at her and stabbing down with her Uin. The Evolent rolled aside, kicking up and into Hayley's side with naniate-enhanced strength. The blow took Hayley by surprise. It was powerful enough to throw her sideways and put some space between them.

"Witchy, let's go," Quark said. "We've got what we came for."

Hayley found Narrl headed for the door, while Quark put down a heavy layer of cover fire from a pair of rifles he had claimed from somewhere.

She glanced back. Tibor was breaking off his attack, headed for the exit. Where was the Gifted?

She found him in the middle of a dozen Servants. His qi was weakening; his naniate stores were depleted. If she left him, he was going to die.

"Witchy," Quark said again.

She looked back. The Colonel was watching her. The Gifted could have killed her, but didn't. Maybe he wasn't an ally, but he also wasn't an enemy.

"Sir, we can't leave him behind," she said, springing back toward him.

She landed beside him, slashing one of the Servants, shooting another, and then removing its head. He glanced at her, then threw his Uin past her, burying it in a Servant's head.

They fought together, just the two of them at first, putting down the group of Servants around them. Then Quark and Narrl started shooting into the thick, clearing the way.

"Come on," Hayley said, bending down and grabbing his Uin.

She could tell by the color and wear on it that it was old. Probably thousands and thousands of years old.

He ran beside her, retreating toward the door.

"Stop," the Evolent shouted behind them.

Hayley could feel her Gift reaching out for the man. She shifted closer to him, putting her arm around his waist, staying close enough to him that the Evolent's Gift couldn't find purchase. It backed off, letting them reach the other Riders.

Quark's qi was shifting colors rapidly, unsettled and angry. The Servants were regrouping, marching back toward them and changing out the magazines in their rifles.

A pair of Planetary Defense drones buzzed by overhead, sweeping down the street and turning around. Hayley could hear ground units coming their way.

"We need to get out of here and find a way back to the spaceport," Tibor said.

"We're going to be surrounded in a minute," Hayley said.

"I know a way," the Nephilim said. His qi was gray and tired. "I used it to get down here almost as fast as you did."

"Lead on, Mister?" Quark paused to wait for a name.

"Mazrael," he replied.

"Cool name," Narrl said.

"Follow me," Mazrael said.

HE BROUGHT THEM DOWN A NEARBY ALLEY AND THEN TO A metal grate in the center.

"Another sewer?" Tibor said. "Ugh."

"Not a sewer," Mazrael said. "A tunnel. It was originally going to be a transportation tube, but the Republic decided to send their armies here, war happened, and it was never finished. Not enough population to make it worthwhile."

"How'd you know it was here?" Narrl asked.

"The same way I knew the Nephilim were here," he replied. "I paid attention."

He bent down, grabbing the grate and using the Gift to help him lift it. He only got it halfway before his strength started giving out, his power spent. Tibor had remained in his second form, just in case, and he picked up the slack, grabbing the grate and helping Mazrael move it aside.

"Everybody in," Quark said, keeping an eye on their backs.

"Quickly," Hayley said.

The Servants hadn't given up. Neither had PD. The group

had a small head start, but it would disappear in a hurry if they didn't stay in motion.

Narrl went in first, his large Curtain frame barely clearing the hole. Mazrael followed after, and then Tibor, Hayley, and Quark.

The tunnel was dark and damp. The grate led to a drain below it, but it had backed up a long time ago and wasn't removing the water as quickly as it was deposited. It left the passage with a nasty smell that made Hayley want to wretch.

"Always a smell," Tibor said. He had to return to his first form to make it through the hole. "Not a sewer, my ass."

"The sewer is under us," Mazrael said. "This way. It won't take them long to figure out we're down here."

There was noone to move the grate back into position.

The tunnel didn't have any lights. They started down it with only the dim illumination filtering in through the open grate, cast into total darkness once it was gone.

Hayley didn't have any trouble without light. As long as she had qi or naniates to fuel her vision, she saw the same regardless. The others weren't as fortunate. They stumbled in the dark until Mazrael created a contained light with his Gift.

They had gone a hundred meters or so when they heard the first of the enemy reach the tunnel opening, jumping in and softly splashing the gathered runoff beneath the hole.

"They're heeeeere," Quark said. "Witchy, take the rear."

"Yes, sir," Hayley replied, sliding past the others to the end of the line. She faced backward, able to spot the silvery flow of the naniates in the Servants behind them.

She watched them bring up their rifles, intending to fire despite not being able to see in the pitch black.

"Get down," Hayley said, dropping herself.

Shots echoed in the darkness, whipping past over their heads. When the Servants didn't hit anything, they stopped shooting, lowering their weapons and increasing their pace forward.

"Too close," Narrl said.

"Don't get shot again," Quark replied. "Or you will be off the team."

"Go ahead," Hayley said. "I'll take care of them and catch up."

"You can't take them all on yourself," Tibor said. "You don't even know how many there are."

"Seventeen," Hayley said, quickly counting them. "Colonel, would you mind loaning me a rifle."

"Gladly," Quark said, passing one of the guns to her. "Don't be long."

"Yes, sir."

She turned back to the Servants while the rest of the group continued ahead, picking up their pace down the long tunnel.

The Nephilim walked toward her, having apparently decided there was nothing in this part of the tunnel to shoot. She waited patiently for them, allowing them to come closer as she shouldered the rifle Quark had given her.

When they were within a dozen meters, she started shooting. Single shots, one quick muzzle flash after another. She moved to another position before the Servants returned fire, peppering the place where she had been standing.

She picked them off, one at a time like she was in a Construct shooting game instead of a smelly tunnel on a Fringe planet. The bullets couldn't bring them down completely, but they could damage the near-zombies enough that they weren't able to hold their guns and fire back.

They kept marching toward her, even as the rounds tore into limbs and knocked the rifles from their hands.

The Evolent dropped into the tunnel at their backs. "There's no reason for me to waste my Gift trying to hurt you, is there Miss Cage?" she said, remaining near the opening to the surface.

Hayley had no indication the Evolent had lit the tunnel, but there was no other way she could have seen her there.

"I guess the word is getting around," Hayley said.

"You should have killed Bale when you had the chance."

"Where is the dog? I'd like to make up for that mistake."

The Evolent laughed. "Still on Kelvar. We have no use for him now. The data chip you took, on the other hand."

"Still after the chip? Forget it."

"We've proven we can find you anywhere you go. No matter what you think you're planning, we've already figured out what comes next. Why not just turn over the chip and move on with your life? You can't win. Not in the long run."

"I admit, you do have an annoying habit of turning up ahead of us. But so what? We have the chip, and we have Pallimo. You have what, exactly? A bunch of zombies? You don't even have your super soldiers anymore. Tell Thetan to keep trying. I'm mildly amused."

"I know what you don't have," the Evolent said. "Your mother."

Hayley's chest tightened, her anger bursting to the surface. She wanted to rip the bitch's face off. She held herself back. She didn't even know if the woman meant Abbie or Nibia.

"Enjoy the rest of your time on Athena," she said instead. "I'm sure we'll be seeing you around."

Then she turned her back on the woman, rushing through the tunnel to catch up.

The Evolent didn't follow.

IT DIDN'T TAKE HAYLEY LONG TO REACH QUARK AND THE others. She would have thought the Colonel had slowed their pace a little, just in case, but she had to believe he had more confidence in her than that. He was simply being cautious, especially in the dim illumination Mazrael's waning Gift provided.

"Our tail is chopped, Colonel," she announced, reaching the back of the line.

"Roger," Quark replied. "Nice work, kid."

"Yeah, good job, Witchy," Tibor said, glancing back at her.

"I had a short convo with Evolent Bitch after I finished disabling the Servants," Hayley continued. "She made a comment about being able to find us anywhere we go before we go there."

"Sounds about right if they're hacked into the HaulNet," Quark said. "Either ours or the Don's movements have all been transmitted through there ahead of time."

"Yes, sir," Hayley said. "But there was something in her qi

when she said it. An arrogant confidence. And didn't Pallimo say they knew the network was compromised?"

"What are you suggesting?"

"I don't know. I just think there's more to this than we've realized yet."

"I know there's more to this than we've realized yet," Quark replied. "But right now, we need to get our asses out of here. We can figure out what we don't know later."

"Yes, sir."

"Mazey," Quark said. "How far to the spaceport?"

"Not much further," the Nephilim replied. "But the tunnel doesn't go all the way there. We'll need to cover the last few blocks in the open."

"Of course, we will," Quark said. "It wouldn't be a party otherwise. Gnarley, you got any rounds left?"

"Yes, sir," Narrl replied. "Nine."

"Fragging great. Witchy, did you burn up the rifle or what?"

Hayley had kept a count of her shots, but she hadn't started with a full magazine. "I'm not sure."

"Tibs, can you check it?"

"Yes, sir."

Tibor took the rifle from her, looking at the readout. "Fourteen, Colonel."

"Roger that. I've got seven. That is painfully low on ammo." He paused. "Shit. Not much we can do about that. Gnarley, you got a blade hiding under the fluff somewhere?"

"Yes, sir," Narrl said.

"See, you can always trust a Curlatin to be prepared. If we're going to get out of this tunnel and off this fragging planet, we may need to bash some heads. Let's try not to kill any of the PD if we can avoid it. Pallimo might be able to smooth all of this bullshit over so long as we don't end any government employees."

"Yes, sir," they replied quietly.

"Mazey, what's your business with Thetan, anyway, that you were doing your damnedest to rain on his parade?"

"It's a long story," Mazrael replied. "Better told in the safety of a starship on its way somewhere else, with a nice bottle of Quirzak Blue to keep things casual."

"Quirzak?" Quark replied. "Only pansies drink Quirzak."

"I like Quirzak," Hayley said.

"You don't count," Quark said. "You're a girl."

"So I'm allowed to like drinks that are too weak for men, sir?"

"Damn right. I bet the Chalandra has Quirzak on it. Pansy drink for a pansy starship. What do you think, Gnarley?"

The Curlatin shrugged. "I've never tasted-"

He was cut off when the ground suddenly shook violently, rattling the tunnel and knocking them off balance. A few seconds later, Hayley heard the deep thump of something in the distance. It was followed by another a few seconds after that. And then a third and a fourth.

"Frag me," Quark said.

"What's happening?" Tibor asked.

"Sounds like heavy artillery," Narrl said.

"Give the teddy a teddy," Quark said. "If I didn't know any better, I'd say they're bombarding the planet from orbit."

The tunnel shook again, causing dust and debris to rain down on them.

"Does that mean they've given up on trying to grab the chip?" Tibor said.

"Nah," Quark replied. "Evolent Bitch must have told their ship's commander we went underground. They're probably hitting the spaceport, knocking out as many of the mercs there as they can and trying to keep us stuck here. They must have hit PD too, to be firing from orbit unchallenged. Thetan's getting bold, attacking Athena like this."

"Or desperate," Tibor said. "Maybe he's not so confident he can track us after all."

"I didn't get that impression from the Evolent," Hayley said.

The tunnel shook again, rattling hard enough that a crack appeared in the synthcrete over their heads.

"Are you sure about not wanting to bury us down here?" Tibor said. "They can kill us and then dig out the chip."

"Only if they can track us," Quark said. He paused and looked at Mazrael. "Which they can, as long as we have a Gifted Nephie with us. Whose Font did you drink from, Mazey?"

Mazrael hesitated to answer. If a Nephilim drank from a Font, they took in the naniates mixed with it. When those naniates belonged to another Nephilim, usually a Venerant, they were bonded to them. Which meant the Venerant could not only track the naniates, but could exert some measure of control over them, even from a great distance.

"Tell me it's Thetan," Quark said.

"It's Thetan," Mazrael admitted.

Quark raised his rifle, putting it against Mazrael's head before he could move.

"Son of a bitch. I should kill you now and save us all the trouble."

"No," Hayley said, pushing past Tibor to get between them. She froze, realizing she was breaking rank. "Sir," she added quickly. "He knew Thetan's Evolent was here. He may have other information."

"You're out of line, Witchy," Quark growled.

"I'm sorry, sir. I don't want us to make any hasty decisions."

Quark stared at her. His qi was mixing red with yellow. He was angry at her for defending Mazrael, and at the same

67

time proud of her for it. He knew she could see it, even if the others couldn't.

"All right, Witchy," he said. "Don't let anyone ever say I don't listen to reason." He lowered the rifle. "He's your responsibility. He frags us over; it's on you."

"Yes, sir," Hayley replied, glancing back at Mazrael.

The Nephilim's qi was grateful. She still didn't see any deceit in it.

"Let's move," Quark said. "We need to get out of this habi-trail and out someplace a little less claustrophobic."

"This way," Mazrael said, breaking into a run ahead of them.

They hurried to follow.

THE GROUND SHOOK TWICE MORE BEFORE THEY REACHED THE end of the tunnel, the force of the blasts knocking them around like rag dolls. The Nephilim were stepping up their bombardment, the increased force and frequency suggesting there was more than one ship firing from space.

The activity raised a lot of questions in Hayley's mind. Questions that had few answers. Foremost: how the frag had Thetan managed to organize enough of a military presence in this part of the universe to have his way with Athena, and nobody, including Don Pallimo, knew anything about it beforehand.

She wanted to ask Pallimo that very question, but the synth was still unconscious over Narrl's shoulder. Or at least, it was pretending to be unconscious. It was probably just as well. Having it alert during their escape would only be a distraction.

Mazrael quickly scaled the ladder leading out of the space, using his Gift to throw the heavy grate aside. Hayley climbed up behind him, moving out into the alley and ducking low, aiming her pistol and spinning around. A quick scan didn't reveal any violent red qi pointed in their direction.

Not that the area was calm. She could hear rifle fire. She could smell burned flesh and charred metal. There was screaming and shouting. The sky wasn't its normal emptiness, but was painted with red and orange streaks of heat energy blasting down toward them.

The ground rumbled, shaking everything, as more screams and shouts went up in response to the latest blast.

"Which way?" Quark asked, pulling himself out of the opening.

"That way," Mazrael replied, pointing.

"Tibs, take point," Quark said. "And do it ugly."

Tibor responded by shifting to his second form, growling in pain as he did. He couldn't change back and forth at will and without pain like a normal Goreshin. There was a price to be paid for his enhanced strength, speed, and healing factor.

He grew bigger and larger, his face and mouth elongating out into a large mouth of sharp teeth, his hands and feet turning into razor claws. His armor grew with him, keeping him modest as he bounded off down the alley on all fours.

"Form up, Riders," Quark said. "Follow that doggie."

They ran after Tibor, who had already turned the corner. Hayley heard him snarling and then a groan from someone nearby. Someone started shooting at him, and when she made it to the corner, she saw the full extent of the chaos.

Planetary Defense was stuck under cover, hiding behind armored transports and doing their best not to be killed. The Nephilim had landed a dropship nearby and unloaded not only soldiers but a pair of mechs. There were bodies littering the streets, mainly PD Enforcers and their drones, mixed in with a few blacksuits. More of the enemy were moving through the streets, and now they were trying to recover from Tibor's unexpected assault.

"Fragging frag me to fragging hell," Quark said, taking in the mess. "This is the worst week I've had since that time I almost got married." He glanced over at Hayley. "Not to Nibia. A long time before that."

He started shooting, firing on the blacksuits. Their heads snapped back as they dropped, one after another until he was out of rounds.

Hayley and Narrl did the same, quickly emptying their magazines. Hayley switched to her Uin as the Nephilim started recovering from their surprise attack.

The mechs down the street began to turn toward them, ready to take on the newcomers. Meanwhile, PD had frozen on their flank. Not shooting at them, but also no longer shooting the Nephilim.

"I need to recover," Mazrael said to her. "I'm too weak like this."

"Recover?" Hayley said. "You mean have a drink?"

He nodded.

"Forget it. You want help getting out of here; you don't do that."

"Do you have another way to stop those mechs?" he replied. "You may be immune to the Gift. Are you immune to heavy lasers?"

One of them fired as he said it, the blast hitting an armored transport the PD soldiers were hiding behind. A huge, molten hole appeared in the side of the vehicle, and the soldiers behind it were vaporized.

"We don't even have any guns," Mazrael added.

Hayley shook her head. She had pretty much asked to be his keeper, and he was already putting her to the test.

The mechs were on the move, lasers firing into the remaining PD transports. Once they were destroyed, the machines would turn their attention to the soldiers on the ground who were scrambling to escape the lasers.

"Close in!" Quark shouted from nearby, ordering the group to get close to the blacksuits and hope the mechs wouldn't fire into their own. That was never a guarantee with the Nephilim.

"Witchy, you know there aren't any other options," Mazrael said. "I can stop them if you let me."

"Why do you want to?" Hayley asked. "I mean, what's in this for you?"

"Vengeance," he replied simply.

She stared at his qi. She turned her head, looking out at the chaos around them. There was a soldier down nearby, his qi dark purple and fading fast. A PD soldier, he had naniates in his system.

"Him," she said, pointing. "Make it fast, and don't expect to do it again while you're with us."

He nodded, already rushing to the dying man. She turned away when he crouched down beside him, sinking his face into the man's neck.

Fragging Nephie Gifted. It was disgusting enough on its own, and her own experience with it made it all the more nauseating.

She shifted her attention back to the fight. Tibor was in the middle of a group of blacksuits, ripping and tearing and biting at them as they tried to get clear shots to shoot him. When they did, the wounds healed within seconds, the pain only making him more angry.

She found Quark, long knife in hand as he laid into the soldiers, getting so close it was hard for them to take a shot at him.

There was Narrl, balancing Don Pallimo on his broad shoulders while lifting one of the soldiers in a massive, furry hand and stabbing them in the gut with a nasty, serrated knife.

Another squad of blacksuits were heading for Mazrael. He couldn't see them in his current situation.

First, she had to let him recover his Gift, and now she had to protect him? She bounced toward him, Uin flashing in front of her as the soldiers opened fire, the rounds hitting the weapon and skipping off. She changed direction and bounced toward them, weapon flashing through hands and necks, her body moving fluidly from one position to another as she danced into the soldiers, cutting them down.

A wash of heat and brightness exploded nearby, an enemy laser flashing into the street less than a meter away, hitting a pair of PD Enforcers who may have been coming to her aid.

They vanished under the intense heat, burned away to nothing.

Something appeared out of the corner of her eye, big and dark. She spun, leading with the Uin, only to have Tibor grab her wrist and stop if from catching him in the head. He grabbed her and leaped away, getting her clear just before a laser hit the ground where she had been standing.

They rolled to a stop together, with the large Goreshin over her.

"Thanks," she said, looking up at him.

"We need to do something about those mechs," he said. "They're firing into their own."

"Working on it," she replied.

He bounced off her, into another blacksuit nearby. She rolled to her feet, looking for Mazrael. She found the body he had been feeding on, but he was gone.

She felt the Gift before she caught it with her vision. It was like a thruster blowing by, a wave of heat that shot past, headed for the mechs.

It was Mazrael, his body moving inhumanely as he

charged the pair of towering humanoid machines, twin Uin in hand and glowing bright red-gold with the Gift.

The lead mech tried to adjust its aim to hit him, a bright flash spearing out from the laser cannon mounted on its arm that crossed only centimeters from the Nephilim's body. He was already moving aside, leaping and rotating and driving toward the war machine.

The pilot swung the mech's arm out, trying to put it between the cockpit and Mazrael. The Nephilim threw his hand out, the arm stopping halfway as it was wrapped in the Gift, frozen in place by the machines.

Mazrael's feet hit the cockpit first, his upper torso swinging forward. He slashed into the glass with his Uin, the Gift and the blades sinking into and through as he slammed into it. It crumbled beneath the blow, and he continued into the cockpit, grabbing the pilot and ripping him from his seat, slicing his neck with the Uin and throwing him out and to the ground.

He fell into the pilot's seat, turning the mech against the other one and blasting it with the first's lasers and chest-mounted machine guns. The other mech wasn't ready for the barrage, and tumbled over, quickly destroyed.

It was a short-lived victory.

A gout of energy poured toward Mazrael's mech from behind a building, a wave of the Gift that made his power look pathetic. It poured into the machine, dissolving its hard, armored shell and sinking in toward the damaged cockpit.

Mazrael jumped awkwardly from the mech, the assault taking him by surprise. He landed hard on his feet and raised the Gift outward, using it as a shield.

The mech exploded behind him, a bright flare of heat and kinetic energy that enveloped him momentarily on its journey away from the center. Hayley raised her Uin and turned away, debris and heat washing past her, the rumble of the detonation deafening.

When she turned back, Evolent Bitch was running toward Mazrael on the strength and speed of the Gift.

He was down, and he wasn't moving.

Hayley charged toward him, using the strength of her lightsuit to almost glide along the surface of the road, her feet barely skipping on the surface before pushing off again.

It wasn't fast enough to reach Mazrael before the Evolent. She came to a stop over him, pulling a blade from her hip and putting the tip against his neck. She hadn't been carrying the weapon earlier.

"Who are you?" she demanded.

She hadn't noticed Hayley coming. Or if she did, she wasn't concerned.

Mazrael didn't respond. He continued to lay there. His qi had been purple when she had hit him, but his body was recovering.

Was he playing dead?

It didn't matter. Hayley reached the scene, her approach finally getting the Evolent's attention. She whirled and brought up her blade, smoothly blocking Hayley's Uin as it swept down toward her. Hayley hit the ground, spinning and kicking, while the Evolent ducked and turned, lashing out with her foot and trying to snap Hayley's ankle. Hayley dragged the foot back and away, balancing on her free foot and driving forward, slamming into the Evolent and pushing her back from Mazrael.

"Didn't expect to see me again so soon, did you?" the Evolent asked, smiling. She shoved back against Hayley, using her Gift to make herself stronger.

Hayley's immunity was worthless against indirect use of the Gift. The strength of the shove knocked her back almost two meters, and she pushed up to go airborne instead of fighting the friction of the earth. She landed, calling out to the naniates and gathering more of them on her tattoos.

She began to glow as she reversed course, charging back at the Evolent. The woman blocked her Uin, meeting her move for move as they danced across the burning city street. Their blades caught again, and their faces pressed close as they pushed against one another with unnatural strength.

"Try that shit again," Hayley said.

The Evolent did, her qi flaring with red-gold energy as she tried to push Hayley away.

Her tattoos flared with blue energy, countering the shove with a push-back of their own. They overpowered the grab, knocking the woman back.

Then Mazrael grabbed her from behind, yanking her head back and sinking his teeth into her neck.

"Mazrael, what the frag?" Hayley shouted.

The Evolent writhed in his grip, trying to break free. Hayley could see the sprout of purple at her back, the other Nephilim's Uin planted firmly in it and holding her in place. He continued to feed on her naniate-enriched blood, gaining millions of the machines with each swallow and adding them to his own.

Gunfire sounded from their right, and bullets started whipping past them. Hayley turned in time to see Quark and

Narrl mow the blacksuits down, having taken rifles from the fallen soldiers.

Then Quark was running toward them, his qi red as hell. He reached them, grabbing Mazrael's head and slamming him to the ground.

Mazrael reached out with the Gift in surprise and self-defense. The flames that burst from his hands washed over Quark without hurting him.

"I'm too pissed for you to hurt me right now, Nephie shit," Quark said. He reached down, grabbing Mazrael by the throat and picking him up.

"Sir, he's on our side," Hayley said. "He didn't mean to attack you."

"I'm. Sorry, Colonel," Mazrael said through a narrow windpipe. "Please."

Quark continued choking him for another second before letting him drop. He grabbed his knife from his belt, turned and ran it through the Evolent's neck, decapitating her in one powerful stroke. Then he spun toward Hayley.

"You need to keep a better eye on him."

"Yes, sir," Hayley said.

"I don't trust him enough to let him get stronger, and neither should you."

"Yes, sir."

"Good. Watch yourself, Mazey. I don't like you Gifted assholes all that much."

"Yes, sir," Mazrael said.

Quark pointed ahead. The spaceport was visible in the distance. A lot of it was already burning, but at least the bombardment had stopped.

"We probably have a few minutes while they figure out who the frag is in charge now," he said, pointing at the Evolent. "Let's not waste them."

They ran, sprinting down the street toward the spaceport.

They were nearly at the terminal when the fire began raining down again. The entrance was empty, save for a few mercs, traders, and blacksuits.

None of them were alive.

They moved out onto the tarmac. A lot of the ships were nothing more than burning wrecks, their crews either dead inside or on the ground nearby. It was a maze of fire and death.

A familiar whine grew in pitch over their heads, a squadron of Shrikes streaking past and firing on positions the bombardment had failed to destroy. Someone was shooting back at them, and more explosions sounded a few seconds later.

Hayley's vision was challenging her, the volume of heat energy around her making it difficult to home in on any details. She could manage her position in relation to the others in the group, but looking in the distance was impossible. She put more attention on sound and smell, but she was dependent on her team to get her back to the Chalandra.

Which was how it should be.

They ran through the smoke and debris, the heat and the destruction. Hayley followed blindly, falling back toward the rear to better use the qi around her. The Shrikes continued to pass overhead, but they mostly ignored them. The wreckage and resulting smoke was good cover, allowing them to move without attracting attention.

"This isn't the way to the Chalandra," Tibor said, his voice deep and gravelly in his second form.

"Nope," Quark replied.

"Where are we going, Colonel?"

"Didn't you check the board before we left for the city?" Quark asked. "We still need a pilot."

"I'm a pilot."

"Barely. There's a squadron of Shrikes overhead, and at

least two battleships up there. You think you can fly us through that bullshit?"

Tibor grumbled, but he wasn't going to admit he could. Not if the Colonel had a better idea.

"Right, so we go this way, and hope we get lucky."

They navigated across the tarmac. The damage got lighter the further they moved from the entrance, the starships around them broken but not destroyed. Their crews were out of their ships, armed and shooting up at the Shrikes when they passed overhead. The mercenaries turned their weapons on them but seeing they weren't in blacksuit they didn't shoot. When everything was going to shit, everybody getting shit on was on the same side.

"Hold up," Quark said, reaching one of the ships.

A group of mercenaries were standing in front of it, shooting lazily up at the Shrikes as they passed. Hayley recognized two of them from earlier. The idiots who had started with Quark.

"Hey, assholes," Quark said.

They turned toward him, and their qi immediately shifted, their fear increasing.

"Who the frag are you?" one of the mercs Hayley didn't recognize said.

"Name's Quark. You?"

"You can call me Captain," he said. "This is my ship and my crew. What the frag do you want?"

"A little politeness wouldn't hurt," Quark said. "I heard you have a pilot. I need her."

The Captain laughed. "You're out of your damn mind if you think I'm giving you my pilot. Jil is my fragging ticket off this planet, once we get the drives functional again."

Quark pointed up at the Shrikes as they swept over again, still shooting. "You better hurry, you want to get out ahead of that bunch."

"It's no concern of yours, Colonel," Captain said, showing he knew who Quark was. "I'll handle my ship; you handle yours."

"I am. I need your pilot. I'm not going to ask again."

Hayley smiled. When exactly had he asked?

"With all due respect, Colonel. You take my pilot; I'm stuck here. So frag off."

"Witchy, go find Jil. I imagine she's passed out in her quarters or something. Get her sober and on her damn feet. We have to move."

"Are you sure the Chalandra's even in one piece, sir?" Tibor asked.

"She has no guns, and the Nephie battleships ought to know it. Why waste energy on a ship that can't shoot back? Witchy, go on. I'll settle the account."

Hayley had a feeling she knew how he would settle the account.

"Roger," she said, walking toward the ramp into the ship.

"Whoa," Captain said, moving to block her. "I didn't give you permission-"

"Permission to kick his ass," Quark said through her comm.

She bounced forward, grabbing Captain's arm and tugging him down, bringing her foot up into his gut. He dropped to his knees, the air knocked out of him. She eyed the other mercenaries, but they didn't move. They had already learned their lesson.

She climbed the ramp into the ship. She could hear Quark behind her, shouting at the Captain.

The ship was a fairly standard VeCorp light cruiser, a common enough pick for a mercenary unit because they were cheap and easy to repair. She didn't need directions to make her way from the exit hatch to berthing, passing a few surprised crew members on her way. They didn't try to stop her, assuming she was there because she was supposed to be.

As she reached the rows of bunks, she heard fresh gunfire outside. It was too loud to be coming from the mercs on the ground, which meant the Shrikes had finished hitting their other targets and were closing on their position.

She had to hurry.

She moved quickly through the bunks, bypassing most of the human-sized beds. Every Trover she had ever seen was between three and four meters tall.

She froze when she heard someone murmuring in their sleep. The translator wasn't able to do anything with it, but she recognized the pitch and tone of the Tro language. She hit the panel on the rack beside her, and the privacy screen slid up.

Trover women were known across the galaxy as being the real brutes of the race. There were hundreds of jokes about them, and all of the male Trovers she had known always made comments about the toughness of their better gender.

Even so, Trover females rarely left their homeworld, and Hayley had never even seen one in any capacity before now.

For one, she was shorter than a Trover male, with a much slighter build, to the extent that she looked almost delicate. She could have almost passed as a human if she wanted. A male, though, not a female. She had no visible rise to her chest to suggest breasts of any kind, and her general features had an androgynously masculine suggestiveness. What gave her away as not human were the less defined features - the flat nose, the smooth ears, the barely-sunken eye sockets. That and the four fingers on her hands. She didn't look like a brute, or a monster, or any of the other things the Trover males called their opposite gender.

Her qi was calm, though it was a sickly yellow with intoxication. She was mumbling in her sleep.

"Jil," Hayley said, putting her hand on the Trover's shoulder.

The female rolled quickly, lashing out with her hand and hitting Hayley in the top of her chest. The suddenness of the attack and the lack of red qi preceding it took her completely by surprise, and she stumbled back and crashed into the bunks on the other side.

"Frag off!" Jil grumbled. "Can't you see I'm trying to get some Zs? Tell Captain whatever it is, it can wait."

"We're under attack," Hayley said. "The whole city is getting pummeled."

"Okay," Jil said. "What the frag do you want me to do about it? Wake me up when it's over, assuming I don't get blasted while I'm sleeping."

Hayley smiled. She liked her attitude.

"Colonel Quark needs a pilot to get the Riders off Athena," she said.

Jil turned her head and finally opened her eyes, looking at Hayley.

"Whoa," she said. "What the frag is with the bubble on your head? You damn near scared the piss out of me, and that wouldn't be pretty." She paused a second. "Did you say Colonel Quark?"

"Yes. I'm with the Riders."

"Shit," she said.

She tried to pull herself out of the rack, getting tangled in her blankets. She was naked underneath, but she didn't seem to care. She fought with her covers, rolling off the edge of the rack and onto the floor.

"Frag," she said. "I think I did just piss myself."

"You're drunk," Hayley said.

"Yeah well, nobody told me the planet was going to get attacked, and Colonel Quark was going to come calling. Of all the shitty days for me to get plastered." She tried to pick herself up. She leaned on the rack, closing her eyes. "Damn, I think I'm gonna-"

Her words were cut off when she vomited on the side of the rack, a stream of half-digested food and bile that smelled worse than any toilet.

Hayley turned her head away. This individual was going to fly them out of here? She would feel better with Tibor at the controls.

"Witchy, any fragging day now," Quark said through her comm. "Shrikes are getting too damn close."

"Roger," she replied. "We're coming. Where are your clothes?"

Jil froze. "What? I'm naked?" She glanced down. "Shit. Who the hell undressed me?" She shook her head. "I don't remember. Maybe I did?" She reached up over her rack, opening her locker. She grabbed a fresh pair of underwear and a flight suit from it.

She tried to put her underwear on and almost fell over. Hayley caught her, propping her up.

"Don't move for a minute," she said.

She put her hand against Jil's forehead. She had to be careful. Naniates were deadly to Trover, and while the machines didn't enter their bloodstream on purpose, she could only sober her up by using them to filter the toxins from her blood. It was a delicate balance, but witchdoctor training took five grueling years for a reason.

She sent the naniates in, a small number navigating carefully through Jil's bloodstream under her control.

"You're going to feel light-headed," Hayley said.

"I already feel light-headed."

She kept her attention focused on the thoughts she was transmitting to the naniates, and on the Trover's qi. She would know if the naniates were doing more harm than good, and she would be able to pull them out.

They moved through Jil's blood, burning off the alcohol in her system. It took almost a minute, and Quark hit her up a couple of times to complain about the delay. There was nothing she could do but ignore him.

Finally, she pulled her hand away. Jil's qi was a clean blue, tinged with streaks of bright yellow.

"Better than sex with a Trover male," she said. "I'll give you that."

"Put your clothes on," Hayley replied. "And meet me outside."

Jil didn't keep them waiting long.

She emerged from her starship in a silver flight suit, a pair of pistols strapped to her hips and her qi beaming with pride at the fact Colonel Quark had asked for her personally.

The Captain was standing with Quark, his mouth shut, his qi slightly gray with upset. Whatever the Colonel had said to him had convinced him not to put up a fight, but it still wasn't making him completely happy.

The Shrikes streaked overhead, firing down into the smoke. Their rounds hit the top of the starship, blasting deep gouges into the armor, and probably through, cementing the fact that the vessel would never see space again.

"Colonel Quark," Jil said, coming to attention in front of him. "Lieutenant Jil reporting for duty."

"You sober, Jil?" Quark said.

"Aye, Colonel."

"Good, then it's time to get the frag out of here." He glanced at the two crew members nearby. "Go tell the others to make themselves scarce. If you survive this shit, put in a call to Don Pallimo. We'll make sure you get paid."

"Yes, sir," they said.

"What's going on, Colonel?" Hayley asked.

"I had to make a deal. We get Jil, but we have to bring Cap here with us."

"You say that like I'm dead meat," Captain said.

"We'll see," Quark replied. "You'll need a new handle, that's for sure. Only one rank in this outfit, and that's me."

"Yes, sir," he replied.

"Chalandra's a few hundred meters that way. Let's hope she's still in one piece."

He started running, the rest of the group running with him. Hayley could hear him muttering under his breath as he moved, and she almost started laughing.

"Stupid pansy-ass starship. Figures I have to be stuck with you for another ride."

The Shrikes crossed over, holding their fire. Hayley wasn't sure why, until a fresh group of blacksuits emerged through the smoke. Except they weren't normal blacksuits.

"Goreshin," Tibor growled, charging the enemy before Quark could give the order.

Each side drew whatever weapons they had. The lead Nephilim soldiers changed to their second form as Tibor reached them. They were almost comically tiny compared to him. They growled and tried to defend themselves, falling quickly to Tibor's furious assault.

"Sweet attack dog," Jil said.

"Damn right," Quark agreed.

The fight was over in a hurry, the Goreshin falling to the Rider's defenses. They continued on, quickly reaching the Chalandra. The smaller luxury cruiser was still intact, though the reflective silver surface had a couple of marks on it from a few close calls.

"This is your ship?" Jil said, horrified.

"It's a loaner," Quark replied, groaning as he opened the hatch. "Just get in and fly her."

"Aye, sir," she said.

"I know you have a reputation, Colonel," Captain said. "But running missions in a pleasure boat? You're crazier than I thought."

"I just said it's a loaner, damn it."

The group piled into the starship. Tibor was bringing up the rear, and he cried out as bullets started peppering the hatch, the rounds finding his back. He tumbled inside, cursing, while Narrl lowered the Pallimo synth to the floor and turned back on the shooters.

"Wait for me," someone said from outside.

Lana was crossing toward the ship from the side, firing on the blacksuits and rushing to the ramp. There was no sign of Kavil.

Narrl laid down cover fire, his big hands gripping the human-sized rifle awkwardly. His aim was impressive all things considered, and he kept the blacksuits at bay while the mercenary scaled the ramp and climbed inside.

Then Hayley hit the control panel to close everything up, the ramp quickly retracting and the hatch sliding closed behind it. The interlock hissed as it sealed.

The engines began to hum, the Chalandra vibrating gently while it powered up.

"Tibor," Hayley said, kneeling beside him. His wounds were already healing.

"I'm okay, Witchy," he replied. "Just need a few minutes."

"Let's hope we live that long," Captain said.

"What happened to Kavil?" Hayley asked.

"Loser," Lana replied. "Killed by PD, and they can't hit the broad side of a cargo hauler."

Hayley didn't like the cold reply, but she nodded.

"Hold onto your asses back there!" Quark shouted.

"We need to get strapped in," Hayley said. The ship wasn't designed for quick escapes, and the nearest seats with buckles were on the main deck up the stairs. "That way."

"I can hold them," Mazrael said. "But you need to take care of yourself."

Hayley nodded, bouncing away and up the stairs. She was thrown into the wall as the ship lifted off the ground and Jil pegged the thrusters. She called out to the naniates, using them to soften the blow when she hit, pushing against the sudden g-forces.

The bridge was a dozen meters forward. She could see the rear of the command station and the heat signatures of the Shrikes beyond it, angling around to get behind the luxury cruiser.

The Chalandra banked hard, and she braced herself, using her Meijo to help remain steady against the momentum, tugging herself forward toward the bridge to get a better seat.

The ship bucked and moved, banking and rolling like an atmospheric fighter, the adjustments in vectoring thrusters and power so deft and smooth she could hardly believe anyone could fly that way. Compared to Jil, Tibor was a clumsy oaf behind the controls.

They angled upward, ascending toward space. The ship had been designed to dampen outside noise, but even so, the reactors whined under the pressure Jil was putting on them, fighting to provide the power she was requesting.

Then the whine suddenly stopped, cutting completely. At first, Hayley thought the reactors had failed, the thrusters had given out, and they were on their way toward an ugly crash.

A moment later, a pair of projectiles shrieked past the cockpit, so close the heat flare in Hayley's vision nearly filled her entire frame. The Chalandra dipped, face down to the planet, now a dozen kilometers or more below.

The thrusters fired on, the energy pushing them downward, competing with gravity to see which could drive them faster into the dirt. Hayley fought to claw her way forward, gaining another meter as the ground approached below.

Then the ship was changing direction, thrusters cutting again as it started to rise, the g-forces ripping at her body and threatening to crush her. The ship leveled out high about the planet, and then the thrusters roared to life again, propelling them horizontal to the ground and back out toward space.

Hayley had a dozen seconds of flat acceleration to pull herself forward to the bridge, passing the open hatch and making it to the side of the command station. Quark glanced over at her, a massive smile on his face.

"Nice of you to join us, Witchy," he said. "Having fun yet?"

"Tons, sir," Hayley replied, allowing herself a smile.

"Better hurry your ass to a seat. We aren't out of this shit yet."

She nodded, making her way to the navigator's station and buckling herself in.

"I hope we didn't pancake the rest of them," he said.

"No, sir. Mazrael is suspending them with the Gift."

Quark made a disgusted face but didn't say anything. He turned his attention back to his station's screens.

The Chalandra started banking again, moving back and forth as it neared the edge of the atmosphere. The Shrikes were still behind them, but their ammunition stores were nearly depleted, forcing the pilots to save their bullets for a clean shot that wasn't coming.

Jil maneuvered the pleasure boat into the thermosphere, the heat shielding glowing as they started to pierce the bubble leading into space.

"Where are the Nephilim battleships?" Hayley asked.

"Good question," Quark replied. "Looks like a few thousand klicks out. Too far away to-"

The ship's sensors started raising the alarm for an imminent collision.

"What the frag?" Quark said.

"Missiles incoming," Jil said, her voice calm. "Nukes from the battleships."

"How the hell? It's like they fired them before we got here. Like they knew exactly where we were going to pull through the atmosphere."

Jil didn't answer. She was too busy trying to keep them in one piece. She did something with the controls that made it feel like all of Hayley's skin was being ripped from her body, and then the nuclear warhead detonated nearby, the resulting EMP pulse reaching out for them.

Another tone sounded on the bridge, and the reactors made an audibly different noise before regaining themselves. A fresh alert sounded as the trailing Shrikes got off a fresh round of fire, bullets pouring into the luxury cruiser's stern.

It was enough that it should have destroyed them, but it didn't. It absorbed the blows more like a military vessel than a pleasure boat, and Jil changed vectors to pull them away from the starfighters.

"Witchy, tell Gant to get us to FTL," Quark said. "I'm done with this shit."

"Yes, sir," Hayley replied, passing the order to the AI.

"Destination?" Gant said.

"The usual," Hayley replied.

"Anywhere but here. My favorite place."

"Mine, too."

"Prepping the disterium drive and calculating coordinates. Standby."

"ETA?" Hayley asked, knowing Quark would ask her.

"Twenty-seven seconds."

She passed the news to Quark.

"Not bad," he replied.

"We can outrun them for that-" Jil started to say, her voice freezing as a form appeared out of the emptiness of space in front of them.

Two forms. A second pair of ships that had been cloaked and waiting for them.

"Shit," Jil finished quietly, already working the controls to get out of their path.

They uncloaked to attack, both of them opening fire on the smaller ship. Plasma poured from large cannons, blobs of superheated gas headed for the Chalandra.

Jil guided the ship back and forth, somehow getting them around the blasts. She reduced thrust, added thrust, and ducked and jived as they closed on the two ships. With Gant already doing the calculations, any major deviation in course would force the AI to start again.

The firepower against them increased, the two cruisers opening up with everything they had. The space around the ship glowed red and orange to Hayley's vision, each flare drawing so close to the Chalandra she could hardly believe they hadn't been hit.

Jil was calm and composed through it all, silent and focused, her hands moving so precisely some of the action was invisible to Hayley, though the ship responded in kind. There was no way parts of the hull weren't getting scorched or scarred, but the shots weren't piercing the hull.

Then they reached the Nephilim ships, aiming to pass directly between them. The guns turned with them, tracking ahead of them and creating a ridiculous field of fire ahead.

Maybe Thetan had given up on the data chip after all.

"Witchy, we need a little help," Quark said.

"Roger," she replied. She had been waiting for him to call

on her. She called out to the Meijo, sending it away from her and out into space. A blue curtain of energy formed on both sides of the ship, the plasma from the cruisers striking it and attempting to break through.

"Ten seconds," Gant said. "Nine. Eight. Seven."

The main thrusters cut out, the disterium reactor taking over and leaving them unable to maneuver. Jil looked back at her, expectantly.

"It isn't going to hold," Hayley said, the pressure against her mind increasing as the naniates protecting them died. She wasn't strong enough. The attack was too intense.

"We're almost there," Quark said. "Come on, kid."

She gritted her teeth, her hands squeezing the sides of her seat as she fought to keep them protected.

It wasn't enough.

The plasma broke through her shield, headed for the port side of the Chalandra, right near the bridge.

Then the bolt slowed until it was hanging in the air as though it had been caught. And it had. Red-gold naniates circled it, keeping it from making contact with the ship.

A blue cloud formed around them, and then the plasma bolt, the Nephilim ships, the Shrikes, and the planet Athena were long gone.

HAYLEY LET HER HEAD DROOP ONTO THE NAVIGATOR STATION'S console. It was pounding from the effort of using the Meijo, her vision spinning through a field of splattered paint she couldn't escape.

"Hoooooooooooooo!" Quark shouted, the effort lasting a dozen seconds. "Hell yeah, Jillie-bean. Whatever I'm paying you, you're getting a raise."

"We haven't discussed terms of my employment yet, sir," Jil said, turning back to look at him.

"Yeah, I guess there hasn't been much time for that yet. I guarantee whatever I pay you, it'll be more than you've made in your life."

"Sounds good to me, Colonel."

"Witchy, you alive over there?"

"Yes, sir," Hayley said. "A little dizzy."

"Nice work, kid. There's nothing wrong with needing a little backup some time."

"That was Mazrael's doing, sir," Hayley said softly. "You wanted to leave him behind."

"Damn right I did. I only don't regret it in hindsight."

Hayley couldn't help but smile at the statement. It was just so Quark.

"How long will we be in FTL?" Hayley asked Gant, before passing the intel back. "Six hours. We're moving toward Koosa."

"All the way? I don't want to lead that asshole Thetan back there."

"No, sir. Just in that general direction."

"Good enough. Jil, you have the bridge. Hal, let's check on Don Pallimo. Hopefully, the damn synth has come around by now."

"Roger," Jil said. She stood to take the command station from Quark when he got up.

Hayley unbuckled herself and stood. Her head was spinning, but she managed not to fall over. Quark's hand was on her arm a moment later.

"I've got you, kid," he said.

He helped guide her from the bridge. The others were already making their way up and were at the top of the plush staircase. The Don Pallimo synth was with them, awake and under its own power.

"Nice of you to join us, sir," Quark said to it. "Your timing is impeccable, as always."

"My apologies, Colonel," Don Pallimo said. "The Evolent shorted my neural pathways. It took some time to reroute and regenerate."

"Neural pathways?" Captain said. He looked at Quark. "This is Don Pallimo, right?"

"Hold up," Quark said. "You need to sign an NDA before we go any further. All of you do, save for Witchy here. Keep in mind, we're already hunting a Rider that betrayed me, and you'll get to see first hand what I do to them when we catch up."

"NDA?" Lana said. "How do we sign?"

"Gant has the docs, don't he, Witchy? Let's just get the NDAs out of the way. We can talk terms later."

"Pardon me, Colonel," Mazrael said. "I'm not interested in joining your group."

"Good," Quark said. "I'm not interested in having you. But, you're stuck with us until we touch down someplace civilized, and places like that have been hard to come by lately. So sign the damn forms, and we'll figure the rest out later. Unless you were planning on killing us all in our sleep?"

Mazrael laughed. "Of course not. The enemy of my enemy is my friend."

"I've heard that before. It doesn't always turn out to be true."

"You can trust me, Colonel."

"Said every lying sack of shit ever. I thought I could trust the female Rider who screwed me over. That didn't work out too good for me."

"I have no reason to want to harm you or yours. My personal anger is directed toward Thetan. I'll sign your form, Colonel, but how do you intend to enforce it?"

"Like I said, you'll see how I handle traitors. Witchy, get it done."

"Yes, sir," Hayley replied. "Gant, can you send NDAs for five new recruits to the closest terminal, and one to the command station on the bridge?"

"Six recruits?" Gant replied. "You do realize the odds of choosing six qualified applicants from a closed pool within a three hour period is only slightly above zero. And I'm talking many, many decimal places here."

"Thank you, Gant," Hayley said. "If I want your opinion, I'll ask for it."

"Hmmph. Docs sent."

"Thank you. Docs sent, sir."

Quark led them to the common area of the Chalandra, a large, comfortable open space complete with a full bar and a full-size stream projector. It was configured for lounging at the moment, but they had already discovered the ship could rearrange the inner walls and decor.

They would never use the secondary configuration.

"I feel like I'm on vacation," Lana said, entering the space.

"You do travel in style, Colonel," Narrl said.

"Temporary," Quark said again. "I was hoping to trade this boat on Athena, but that didn't work out so well."

He approached the projector, opening a space on the wall where the control pad was located. He tapped on it a few times, and then called each of the new passengers over in turn. They quickly signed the promises of secrecy without reading the agreement. Non-disclosure agreements were hard for most to enforce.

Quark and the Riders weren't most.

Lana was the last to sign. She ran her finger across the control pad to add her signature, and then Quark snapped the panel closed and turned to them.

"I'll spare you my usual speech to newbies," he said. "For the sake of time and my sanity. As of this moment, you're all on your way to becoming full-fledged Riders. You may be wondering where all of the other Riders are at the moment. You may be wondering where our ship is. The answer is simple: the crew is dead. My ship was destroyed. I came this close to losing everything." He spread his fingers a few centimeters apart. "You can draw your own conclusions on where that puts my mindset at the moment."

The truth that Quark's Riders had been nearly wiped out caused spikes of fear in all of the recruits. Hayley could tell by their qi they were wondering if they made a mistake joining them.

"Don't get all scared on me," Quark said, recognizing their apprehension. "Like I said, we were betrayed. You all don't screw one another or me over; we'll be just fine. Now, we'll discuss payment and benefits later. You're all the best of the best, or at least you managed to survive long enough to make it here, so I'm assuming you're pretty good. I shouldn't need to hold your hands as the shit gets real."

"The shit isn't real yet, sir?" Lana asked.

"Damn right it is, good call, Private."

"Private?" she said.

"Everybody starts as Private on my boat," Quark said. "You need to earn your rank like Jil did. She's already promoted to Lieutenant. How do you like that?"

The crew was silent. They didn't like it, but they were smart enough to know Quark didn't care.

"Private Captain," Captain said. "It'll work."

"Ahab," Quark said.

"What?"

"Your handle is Ahab from this moment on."

"Why?"

"He was a Captain. And an idiot. The shoe fits."

Ahab sighed. "Yes, sir."

"Moving on," Quark said, turning to Don Pallimo. "This here is Don Pallimo. The richest man in the galaxy. But it isn't really Don Pallimo. This one's a synth."

The group's qi registered their surprise and disbelief. Both that they had rescued Don Pallimo, and that he wasn't the real deal. The synth's organic components were more advanced than anything else on the market, making it indistinguishable from real flesh and blood.

"A pleasure to meet you all, I'm sure," Pallimo said.

"We risked our lives for a fake?" Ahab said.

"No, we risked our lives for what the real Don sent the fake to tell us," Quark said. "In case you haven't caught up yet, there are some bad assholes out there looking to cause some serious turbulence in the state of our universe. Witchy, show them the goods."

Hayley dug the data chip out of a tightpack. She had been carrying it the entire time. She held it up.

"This is what they're after. You saw my Goreshin friend Tibs out there. He's the weakest of the patrol dogs the Nephilim want to produce. This chip has the instructions to make them."

All eyes turned to Tibor. He had switched back to his first form, but they had seen him in action. Their qi was white with fear.

"Needless to say, between the betrayal, the murder of my crew, especially my wife and Witchy's mom, and the fact these assholes are now assaulting planets, we've got our work cut out for us. Any questions so far?"

Quark paused a moment. Narrl's hand slowly went up.

"Bob Gnarley, what have you got?" Quark asked.

"If these Nephilim are fragging with genetics, I have a feeling they're doing more with it than making bigger dogs."

"That wasn't a question," Lana said.

"Yes, it was," Narrl said.

"It was a question in the form of a statement," Ahab said.

"Whatever," Quark said. "You're right about that, Gnarlsey-bub. They've got super soldiers. They're working on super-intelligence."

"That's what I wanted to talk to you about, Colonel," Pallimo said. "That's why I set up the meet."

"Do tell," Quark said. "Because I thought you had figured out which bitch turned us over to Thetan."

"I'm still trying to track that information down. No, this is about Project Uplift."

"Uplift?"

"It was the Republic's first real genetic engineering

program. Their goal was to implement an exponential increase in intellect, with the idea that it would allow them to win the arms race against the Outworlds, and finally come up with something that was more versatile than the Shrike."

"You seem to know a lot about it," Quark said.

"I should. I helped fund it."

"What?" Hayley said. "You live in the Outworlds."

"I do, my dear," Pallimo said. "And I never had any intention of letting the Republic taste the ripened fruits of their labors. But I did want the research, and I did want to see what they came up with."

"What did they come up with?" Mazrael asked.

Pallimo walked over to where Hayley was standing. He reached out, tapping on her visor. "His name is Gant," he said. "Well, that's what most Gants call themselves off-world. His real name is too hard to pronounce. He made this for Hayley. It's probably one of the most advanced pieces of technology in the galaxy."

"Wait a second," Hayley said. "You funded the research that made Gant smart?"

"Yes, my dear. In part."

"The facility was burned," she said. "All traces of its existence wiped. Did you have anything to do with that?"

"Yes. When I realized how the scientists had developed the enhancement, I had no choice but to get them to shut the project down."

"And how was the enhancement developed?" Mazrael asked.

"Naniates, of course," Pallimo said. "The Blood of the Shard. The Creator of the Universe. I don't know where they got it, but they were learning to manipulate it. I wasn't aware of the origins of the naniates at the time, but I recognized what they were at a basic level. I also recognized they were too advanced to be from our galaxy. That's what made them dangerous."

"Gant doesn't have any naniates in him," Hayley said.

"No. The Gants as a race are highly resistant to them. Some Seraphim believe they were the first of the intelligent races the Shard created. When they tried to give him the naniates, his body reacted. It was very similar to your experience."

"But he got super-intelligence, and I got blinded," Hayley said. "How the hell is that fair?"

"You aren't blind, Hayley," Pallimo said. "You see all living things for what they truly are."

"Not all the time."

"Nothing is perfect."

"I'd rather be able to see like everyone else. Like I used to. I can't even remember what people looked like anymore. I don't remember the face of my father."

"You also have enhanced senses of hearing and smell, and your external control of the naniates is unparalleled."

"Because of this," she said, touching the visor. "And because they fear me."

"Who cares what the reasons are?" Pallimo said. "You're unique in all the universe. That's something to be proud of, not ashamed of."

"I didn't say I was ashamed. I said I got the raw end of the deal. I'd be more useful if I could see."

"I disagree. How many lives have you saved because of your vision and control?"

Hayley didn't respond right away. Damn it, he was right. "More than zero."

"I appreciate the heart-to-heart," Quark said. "But can you get to the point, sir?"

Pallimo turned back to the Colonel. "The point is, you said the Nephilim were using the Republic's research to further their own. Which means the Nephilim must have found the abandoned facility. They also must have found something in it that the burn team missed. They may have even reinstated the laboratory there, who knows? I thought it was lost and forgotten."

"And you know the location," Quark said.

"I do. I couldn't risk leaving a package for you. Not when I was certain the Nephilim were tracking me. The only option to ensure the information only passed between me and you was to become the package."

Quark laughed. "Good thinking, sir."

"I'll enter the coordinates into the navigation systems myself," Pallimo said. "That way there can be no interference. It will be impossible for the Nephilim to know we are heading their way."

"Sounds damn good to me."

"Good." He motioned toward the bridge. "Shall we?"

"Hell yeah."

16

THEY DROPPED THE CHALANDRA FROM FTL, TOOK A FEW minutes while the Pallimo synth updated the nav computer with the coordinates for the old research facility, and then got the pleasure boat back underway.

It was a ten-hour hop from their current location to the planet in question; a world Pallimo called Yeti-4 because it was a cold-as-hell ice world. Being a Curlatin, Narrl seemed excited by the destination. The rest of the group wasn't looking forward to freezing their asses off.

The short break gave the new Riders a chance to get settled. The ship had enough cabins for everyone to get their own, and for the short ride between Athena and Yeti-4, it was good enough. The only dictate Quark had handed down was that they were not to sleep in the beds under any circumstances. He didn't need his soldiers getting too comfortable.

Hayley was tired. Her use of the Meijo to protect the Chalandra from the Nephilim plasma had weakened her mind, and the action on the ground had exhausted her body.

At the same time, the forward movement in their goals gave her a sense of dulled excitement. It would have been better if all of the original Riders were here, trying to stop the Nephies from ruining the galaxy.

Avenging them was the next best thing.

She was tired, but she wasn't ready to pack it in and claim some downtime. She had questions, and she wanted answers.

Quark had put Mazrael in the room next to hers, to make it easier for her to keep an eye on him. The Colonel was fairly certain the Nephilim wouldn't make trouble while they were in FTL because it would mean his death along with everyone else's. That didn't mean he trusted the Gifted.

They were an hour into the journey when Hayley knocked on the door to his cabin. She had showered again and changed, swapping out her lightsuit for workout clothes. She wasn't planning on hitting the gym, but she preferred the feeling of the material against her flesh, as opposed to something loose and baggy.

The hatch slid open. Mazrael had used the Gift to activate the controls from across the room. He was settled in on a leather couch with overly thick cushions, a gold mug filled with fresh coffee in his hand. The serving bot was holding the tray and the rest of the pot behind him.

"Coffee?" the Nephilim asked.

She entered the cabin. He had claimed one of the suits they had found inside the closet. It had a high collar and belled sleeves. She could only see the outline of it in his qi, but to her, it looked ridiculous.

"Sure," she said.

The serving bot immediately lifted the pot and began pouring.

"No visor?" Mazrael asked.

"I don't wear it all the time," she replied, crossing the

cabin to the bot and taking the offered cup. "I thought it would help keep things more casual."

"Mi casa es su casa," he said.

"What?"

"Your translator didn't get that? I suppose it's considered a colloquialism nowadays. My house is your house."

"Don't you mean, my house is your house?" she asked.

"I suppose I do." He smiled, amused. He took a sip of his coffee. "Nothing but the best on this ship."

She tasted the brew. "It is good," she agreed.

"I'm assuming you stopped by because you have questions."

She almost said damn right, but she stopped herself. She was spending too much time too close to the Colonel. "That's right."

"Have a seat," he said, motioning to the chair beside the couch. It matched the one in her room, but she hadn't tried it yet. They looked too comfortable.

She slipped into it, sighing softly as she sank into the cushions. "This is nice."

"Would you like something to eat?" the serving bot asked.

"What do you have?" Hayley replied.

"The cabins are stocked with a number of non-perishable delicacies from around the galaxy. Would you like to sample Rudinian Flek?"

"What is it?"

"The Flek is a parasite that grows inside the anus of-"

"No thank you," Hayley said. "I'm not hungry right now."

"Of course, ma'am."

"Good call," Mazrael said.

Hayley didn't want to lean forward in the seat, but she was going to fall asleep right there if she didn't.

"First question," she said. "Who the hell are you?"

He smiled. "I'll give you the short version because the

long one will take days. My name is Mazrael. A long, long, long time ago, I was one of the Shard's original crew members. I fled with Lucifer during the rebellion. I was one of his original twelve, and I helped found the Prophetic that Gloritant Thraven once controlled."

"Bullshit," Hayley said. "That would make you ten-thousand years old."

"Older than that," Mazrael said. "Yes."

"But an Evolent can knock you down?"

"What does age have to do with power? Oh, I've had a long time to increase the density of my Gift. And there have been times when perhaps I've been the most powerful Nephilim in the universe. More powerful than Lucifer, even. But some uses of the Gift burns it irreplaceably."

"Fine, but how have you managed to live so long? Regen treatments are only a few centuries old."

"You see life force, don't you? Qi. You can't see into me."

"And other energy. Heat. Motion. Radiation. Light if it's focused, like a laser. Naniates."

"It's an intriguing way to view the universe."

"It isn't as cool as it sounds. I don't even know what I look like. Not really. Do you think I'm pretty?"

"What do external appearances matter, Hayley? The flesh is a blanket over our souls. What is your soul like?"

"Do you have a soul?" she countered. "You sided with Lucifer against the Shard. You betrayed him when he trusted you. The Extant is a violent place."

"And this galaxy isn't? I was violent in my youth. Angry. We were deceived by the Shard. Whether you believe that or not, it's true."

"Whatever. Ancient history, right? How have you survived so long?"

"What you see looks human to you, doesn't it?"

She nodded.

He put down his coffee and then held out his arm. He picked up one of his Uin from the table and flicked it open.

Then he cut off his hand.

"What the frag?" she said, jumping to her feet.

There was no blood. His qi wasn't purple. It was as though he hadn't been damaged at all.

He held the hand up. "Are you familiar with the Hursan?"

She nodded. "They're symbiotic protozoa."

"Each cell contains its own complete ecosystem. When those cells join together, they create a whole."

"You're a Hursan?"

"No. But one of the genetic seeds we took from the Shard was that of the Hursan. I worked with Lucifer to create the Nephilim races. I used that seed to help him create the Goreshin, like Tibor. And to turn myself into this."

He took the hand and put it back on his wrist. He was whole again within seconds.

Hayley stared at the hand, finding the whole thing hard to believe. "You created the Goreshin?"

"Essentially. To answer your next question before you ask it, that's my issue with Thetan. He's dabbling in science he doesn't understand, with an outcome for this entire universe he doesn't understand. There's a reason Lucifer stopped creating new races when he did. There's a balance to these things, and he's going to destroy it. Short term, he may get the control he wants, but over time, it will be the ruin of everything."

"Is that why you changed sides?"

"What do you mean?"

"You use Seraphim Uin as weapons. I assume you changed sides at some point."

"Not exactly. I was in love with a Seraphim woman. She taught me how to use the Uin. She never knew I was Gifted, never mind a Nephilim."

"You never told her?"

"No. I wanted her, and she would never have wanted me if she knew."

"But-"

"It was many years ago. Age might not bring power, but it does bring wisdom. I know it was wrong."

"What was her name?"

"Charmeine."

"I like that name."

"Me, too."

"If you say I've changed sides, then I've only changed to my own side. I've lost interest in the war between the Seraphim and the Nephilim. My goal is to stop Thetan from his research before he does something that can't be undone."

"Like freeing the naniates?"

Mazrael laughed softly. "Yes. It could be that it's already too late. That we're destined to meet our end. Only time will tell, I suppose."

"Whether we are or not, I have my reasons for wanting to find Thetan."

"I know. We're allies."

"For how long?"

"As long as it takes. Not one minute later. It isn't personal. I see a strength in you that I admire. But my fate is to be alone."

"That sounds sad."

She watched his qi. It had remained a level blue the entire time, so much so that she had a distinct feeling he was manipulating it to keep her from seeing the truth of him.

What was he hiding?

"My future is sorrow," he replied. "For the misdeeds I have done, and the chaos I have wrought."

Hayley was silent at first, not sure what to say. She took another sip of the coffee but didn't sit.

"Are you capable of dying?" she asked.

"Anything that lives is capable of dying," he replied. "I would need to lose most of the cells in my body to prevent them from regenerating."

"What about if someone takes your head?"

"Not enough," he replied. "It would take time, but it would regenerate."

It was gross and amazing at the same time.

"In that case, I'm glad you're on our side."

"As am I," he said. "I like you. I wouldn't want to have to hurt you."

She put her coffee mug down on the serving bot's tray. "That's all I had for now. I'm going to get some rest. I'm totally beat."

"Sleep well, Miss Cage."

She smiled at him and retreated from his room and back to hers. She shivered as she did. She had asked the questions she wanted to ask, and now she was starting to regret it. Besides watching him remove and reattach his hand, there was something about his answers that wasn't sitting quite right. Add in the flatness of his qi, and she was sure there was something there.

She went to her bed, feeling the plush gel mattress before grabbing the pillow, dropping it onto the floor, and lying down. She wanted to trust Mazrael. He had saved their lives. Was the reason she couldn't because he was a Nephilim?

Or was it something else?

17

HAYLEY WOKE UP TO A KNOCK ON HER CABIN DOOR. SHE grabbed her visor and pulled it on.

"Gant, what time is it?" she asked.

"T-minus two hours, Witchy," he replied.

She sighed in relief. She hadn't overslept again.

But then, who the hell was knocking, and why?

The knock came again as she rose to her feet. "Can you get that?" she shouted to the serving bot.

"Yes, ma'am," it replied, heading for the door and hitting the control to open it.

Hayley recognized Don Pallimo's lack of qi immediately.

"Don Pallimo," she said. "I wasn't expecting you."

"I'm sorry to bother you, my dear," Pallimo said. "But I thought you might be interested in heading down to the fitness bay with me."

"What do you need the fitness bay for?" she said.

"I don't, of course. But it seems the Colonel and Tibor made a wager earlier?"

Hayley smiled, remembering the bet the two had made on

Athena. It was the perfect event to get the new Riders integrated and feeling like a single team.

"Thanks. I'll be there in a minute."

"I'll wait."

Hayley used the bathroom and spent a minute brushing her hair flat and putting it back into a short tail. Then she rejoined the Don, walking the short distance to the fitness bay with him.

The crowd was on the outside of the room, on the outside of the double-wide hatch. Only Quark and Tibor were in the bay, standing in the center of the padded floor. All kinds of fitness equipment surrounded them, from the latest in stationary muscle stimulators to old-fashioned adjustable anti-gravity bars.

"Witchy," Jil said, seeing her approach. "You almost missed the main event."

"I've got twenty sats on Tibor," Captain said. "No way he loses to the Colonel."

"You're out of your fragging mind," Lana said. "This is Quark. The Quark. He's a legend for a reason."

"In part, because he chooses the right squad mates; isn't that right, Witchy?"

Hayley nodded. "At least part right."

"Who do you think is going to win?" Narrl asked.

"To be honest, I think it's going to be close either way." She shifted her head. "Has anyone seen Mazrael?"

"I invited him," Don Pallimo said. "He very politely declined."

"His loss," Narrl said.

"All right, Riders," Quark said, turning his attention to them. "Just for a little backstory, old Tibs here doesn't like me calling him Tibs. He thinks it makes him sound like a pansy, instead of a big scary doggie." He looked back at Tibor, smiling. "So we made us a wager. He wins, he gets to

111

pick his handle. I win, he's stuck with Tibs." He paused for effect. "Or worse."

"Riiidddeerrrs," Hayley shouted, cueing the others.

"Riiidddeerrrs," they replied.

"Not bad for your first time," Quark said.

"What are the rules, sir?" Tibor asked.

"Only one rule, my friend," Quark said. "No injuries Witchy can't heal, which means no death. Roger?"

"Roger."

"And try not to destroy the ship in the process."

"Yes, sir."

"Witchy, you want to call it?"

Hayley moved through the group to the front, entering the bay and standing off to the side. Tibor took the opportunity to change to his second form, growing almost too tall for the space to contain him.

"There goes my handicap," Quark joked, cracking his knuckles. "I owe you this beating from Kelvar, anyway."

"That wasn't my choice," Tibor said.

"Don't care," Quark replied. "It is what it is."

"Are you two going to stand there and chat all day, or are you going to fight?" Hayley asked. "I missed an extra hour of sleep for this."

"Sorry, Witchy," Tibor said.

"Call it, then," Quark said.

Hayley raised her hand. Quark and Tibor both crouched into combat stances.

She lowered her hand and shouted, "Fight!"

They didn't waste time circling one another. Quark and Tibor both charged in headlong, grappling together in the center of the room. Only for a moment, though. Tibor overpowered the Colonel, throwing him sideways and into the wall.

Quark hit hard, dropping to the floor and rolling to his

feet as Tibor closed in. He ducked a claw, coming up and hitting the Goreshin with a hard uppercut. Tibor laughed, kicking Quark back to the middle of the room.

"Sorry, Colonel," Tibor growled. "You don't stand a-"

Quark produced a pistol from his pants, shooting Tibor in the chest. It took him and the onlookers by surprise. They cheered while Tibor stumbled back, the wound healing.

The Colonel pulled his knife as Tibor approached, using the surprise to slash across his chest. Tibor hopped back, avoiding it, throwing another punch that Quark ducked under. The Colonel spun and leaped, connecting with a hard punch in Tibor's temple that caused him to stumble.

"Shit," Lana said. "Come on, Tibs!"

Tibor shook off the blow, barely managing to get his hand up as Quark slashed at him again. The blade dug through his palm, sending blood across the mat.

The Goreshin's qi turned yellow-green with surprise. "Poison?" he said. "That's cheating."

"I said there aren't any rules save nobody dies," Quark replied.

"But we have a mission in two hours."

"You should recover by then."

Tibor growled, slashing at the Colonel, attacking with a fresh fury that drove Quark back. His claws were blurs, his movements ferocious. He managed to break through Quark's guard, catching him in the face with his claws and leaving a nasty gash across the Colonel's cheek, opening it from the left side of his mouth to his ear.

He drew up at the damage. "Oh, shit, Colonel," he said. I'm so-"

Quark barely flinched. He used the hesitation to stab Tibor in the chest, pushing back and knocking the Goreshin to the ground, coming down on top of him and planting his knee against Tibor's throat.

"You give up," Quark said. The words were muddled by the damage to his face.

"Yes," Tibor replied, his breathing labored. His qi was a dark purple on the blade and fading.

"Colonel, you're killing him," Hayley said, rushing toward them both. It had been entertaining at first, but the whole thing had turned into a violent, disgusting display of machismo.

Quark pulled the knife out, standing and backing up. "Fix him," he said. "I'll wait." He grabbed a towel from the side of the room, putting pressure on his wound.

Hayley glared at Quark and then knelt beside Tibor.

"Hold on, Tibor," she said.

"Fragging asshole," Tibor said. "It wasn't supposed to be so serious."

"I know. He's pissed about Nibia and the Riders, and he took it out on you. I'm sorry."

She put her hand to the stab wound, pushing the naniates out into it. She didn't have time to get a poultice, which meant she was going to be weakened too. He was the Colonel so she couldn't say anything to him, but she wanted to punch him in the face for being so reckless.

She focused on Tibor instead, healing his wound and burning off the poison. It left her light-headed as she walked over to Quark to fix his face.

"That was stupid, sir," she said under her breath so the others wouldn't hear. She was too angry to stay silent.

"Don't tell me how to run my ship," he replied.

His qi was red. She didn't push any harder. She focused on healing him instead, guiding the naniates into his wound. They knitted him back together, leaving him with a small scar in the corner of his lip, and leaving her exhausted again.

At least she had two more hours to sleep.

Quark moved past her without a word, approaching

Tibor. He stopped in front of the Goreshin, sizing him up. Then he smiled.

"You have all of my respect today, Sergeant," he said, giving Tibor a new rank just like that. "You're a tough son of a bitch and my kind of Rider. You give yourself your own handle. You've earned it."

Tibor looked back at him. He nodded, smiling. Hayley could tell it was fake. He was still mad at the Colonel.

"Just call me fragging Tibs, if that's what makes you happy. I don't care."

Then he turned and stormed out of the bay, pushing past the others.

A tense silence hung over them.

"Well," Lana said sarcastically. "That was fun."

18

Hayley wasn't sure whether to chase after Tibor or wait to get Quark alone and make her opinion known. She decided to chase after Tibor, knowing the Colonel probably didn't care what she thought anyway.

The Riders went their separate ways, most returning to their cabins. Narrl stayed behind to work out, while Don Pallimo retreated to the bridge. The synth didn't need to sleep.

She headed to Tibor's cabin. It wasn't far from hers, though it was a lower tier, which in this case meant it didn't have its own serving bot and was a few square meters smaller. She knocked on the door.

Tibor didn't answer. Was he sulking? Pouting? She waited a minute and knocked again.

The door opened. Tibor was in his human form. His shirt was off. There was a scar where Quark had stabbed him.

"Hal," he said before she could say anything. "Don't. Don't make excuses for him. Don't try to make me feel better." He put his hand on the scar. "This is bullshit. You know it. I know it. I made that wager with him in fun, not to wind up almost dead."

"He told you the rules."

"I didn't think he was serious. When he shot me, that was a little over the edge, but I figured he knew I would heal. But poison? Fragging poison? Do you know how much that stuff hurts?"

"He couldn't have beat you any other way."

"Don't you think I know that? Hell, everyone on this ship knows that. So what?"

"So he couldn't let himself look bad in front of the greenies."

"No excuses, remember? Or you can go away."

"Can I come in?"

He stared at her, sighed, and moved aside.

She entered his room. It looked like it had barely been used. "What do you want to do now?" she asked him.

"What do you mean?"

"You came along because you said you owed me," she replied. "Quark can say what he wants, but you aren't officially a Rider. You didn't sign a contract. You aren't getting paid. You don't have to do a damn thing he says. He'll keep you locked up in here if you refuse to play along, but that's the worst he can do."

"I still owe you for saving my life," he said. "That hasn't changed."

She smiled. "We both know that whole thing is becoming a joke. You've saved my life a few times already, but there's always a reason why you didn't."

He shrugged. He knew he couldn't lie to her. "You're the first friend I've ever really had. I'm not about to abandon you, especially now. And I have as much reason to want to get Thetan as anyone. The torture he put me through." He paused, his qi fading to white with fear. "It makes Quark's bullshit a speck of dust on the galaxy's ass."

"So what do you want to do? Sit in here and cry about it? Or come out stronger?"

He stared at her. "I'm not crying about it."

"But that's what it looks like to the others. You lost, you got pissy, and you stormed off. Quark told you the only rule was nobody ends up dead. Neither of you are dead. I know what he did was lousy, and I know from his qi that he knows too, but he'll never admit it. He had to show the recruits he's still a badass. But he's old, and even regen treatments can only take him so far. He's slowing down."

"Excuses, Hal."

"It doesn't matter. The only one here who looks bad to them is you. Shit, the Colonel promoted you to Sergeant, which means you'll be leading a squad on the next drop. Is this the first impression you want to make?"

That seemed to break him out of his original thought pattern. He froze, shaking his head. "Frag, no."

"Then put your shirt on and get your ass out there. Go back to the fitness bay and work out. Let them see you shaking it off."

He nodded, walking over to the couch where his shirt was neatly folded. He put it on and went back to her. "I'm going to exercise. You want to come?"

She shook her head. "I need to grab whatever extra rest I can get. It was still stupid of Quark to burn me this way, especially since I didn't have my poultices on me or time to get them. I'm pissed at him, too, if it makes you feel any better."

"It does."

He was going to walk past her. She reached out to him, offering a hug. He took it.

"Thanks for everything, Hal," he said.

"You're welcome. Oh, and think of a handle."

"Why don't you give it to me? I've never been good at that stuff."

"Xolo," she replied.

"What is it?" he asked.

She smiled and winked at him, amused with herself. He would either be mad at her when he discovered the origin, or he would think it was hilarious and fitting.

"You'll have to do your own investigation," she said.

"Can I have a hint?"

"It's an Earth word."

"It isn't the name of a clown, is it?"

She laughed. "No. No clowns."

"Then Xolo it is. I'll see you later."

"Roger that."

They both left his cabin. He headed back toward the fitness bay, while she retreated to her room.

Quark was inside when she arrived, sitting on her couch. His presence surprised her.

"Colonel?" she said.

"We're in private, kid," he replied.

"Dad," she corrected, dropping all of the formality. "What's up?"

"I'm old."

She walked over to where he was sitting, plopping onto the sofa next to him. "You've been old for two centuries already. Stars are hot; the universe is cold. What else is new?"

He looked at her. She could see the remorse in his qi. "I went too far."

"I know."

"I didn't have a choice."

"I know."

He was silent for a moment. "I've never been through this shit before," he said. "Captured twice. Losing my grip.

119

Having to pull out all the stops to win a damn brawl. Questioning myself."

"It's been a rough week."

"Damn right. But it's more than that, kid. I'm feeling it. In my bones. In here." He put his hand on his chest. "I never used to feel anything."

"Bullshit," she replied. "I can see what you feel, remember?"

"Fair enough. I've always been able to contain it."

"And now you can't?"

"That's how it feels. Like I'm ready to fragging burst. Like I'm losing my edge."

She leaned over, putting her head on his shoulder. He tilted his head over to press against the top of it.

"Like it or not, Dad, you're still human. If you want to have no emotions, let Pallimo make a synth version of you."

He laughed. "You know, that might not be a terrible idea. Live forever, have lots of copies. I could run multiple teams, spend the night with multiple women."

She punched him in the arm. "Stop it."

"I'm no innocent, kid."

"I know. But you're no heartless asshole, either."

He was silent for a minute, keeping his head close to hers. She was enjoying the moment of closeness. They didn't get enough of them.

"I know you get pissed at your mom sometimes," he said. "Abbie, not Nibia. I know you think she should be around, and she isn't."

She picked up her head. Why was he bringing her up? She didn't want to talk about her mother.

"Dad-"

"No. Just listen for a second. I know for a fact that neither of your mothers would have ever left you without a good reason. Abbie had a lot of responsibility, but most of all to you. The hardest thing for her to do was send you away with me and to stay away to make sure you got to grow up as normal as possible. Frag, I can't even imagine doing the same thing. When I picture you being somewhere else, and I can't see you or talk to you, or something happens to you. Well, you can see it."

She could. His qi was pained. Gray and red and purple and white. It was a mental and physical reaction.

"And I've only known you seven years. And I didn't punch you out from between my legs. You get what I'm saying?"

She nodded.

"I could never stop you from being a soldier," he said. "Abbie said you had always wanted to be like her, and I wasn't going to get in your way. But things are changing, kid. Thetan, he's bigger than anything I've had to deal with in a while, and like I said, I'm old. We'll kick his ass, but I want to make sure you go into battle without that anger at your mom. I want to make sure you have all that anger to use against that Nephie asshole that killed your other mom. You get what I'm saying?"

"I think so."

He nodded, leaning forward to stand. "Good. Get some sleep. I don't say this very often. Shit, I don't know if I've ever said it before, but I'm sorry for what I did to Tibs. There ain't many good Nephies, but he's one of them."

"Xolo," Hayley replied.

"What?"

"He told me to give him his handle. It's Xolo."

Quark started laughing. "You didn't."

"I did."

"You got a touch of your oldest man in you, kid."

"Damn right."

He leaned forward and kissed her on the forehead. "You have an hour. Don't waste it."

"Yes, sir."

Quark left the cabin. Hayley sat on the couch for a few minutes, staring at the door. He had always softened around her, but never that much. It was good to see, and concerning at the same time.

They were all going to need their edges to be as sharp as possible for what was coming next.

HAYLEY WAS ON THE BRIDGE WITH QUARK, DON PALLIMO, AND Jil when the Chalandra came out of FTL, moving back into regular spacetime and pushing through the blue haze of the disterium gas. Yeti-4 was still a short distance away, the coordinates the Pallimo synth had entered giving them ample time to survey the area and bug out if the conditions were lousy.

"What have we got?" Quark asked. He was standing beside the command station.

Don Pallimo had claimed the main operational console since it was remaining behind when the combat team disembarked.

"Clear," Pallimo said. "As expected. There's no way Thetan could have known I knew about this place."

Hayley couldn't see the ice world in the forward viewport, but she could imagine what it looked like. A solid white blob against the black backdrop of the galaxy. Not really that exciting from a distance.

"Why'd you set up shop out here?" Quark asked. "Looks like a shitty place to live."

"It is," Pallimo agreed. "But it also has built-in security. The experiments go wrong, something nasty escapes, where are they going to go? Who are they going to hurt?"

"Fair enough. Jil, you've got the Chalandra once I'm off the bridge."

"Not Don Pallimo?" Jil asked, looking back.

"Nope. He's a civvie, and this is a military drop. I'm sure he agrees."

"Affirmative, Colonel," the synth replied. "I'll assist in any way you deem necessary, Lieutenant."

"Roger," Jil said.

Quark turned to Hayley. "Witchy, let's get our greenies ready for action. I hope they packed some thermals on this pansy ship."

"Me, too," Hayley replied.

They left the bridge, heading to the common area. Most of the new Riders were already there, watching streams and playing games while they waited. Hayley could see their qi mixing and merging in her vision. There was a definite tension to their actions. A line of nervousness and excitement and fear. There hadn't been time to stop and reload anywhere before their arrival, so their level of readiness was already way beyond anyone's comfort level.

Excluding Mazrael. He was sitting in the corner, quiet and confident. The Gift made him a powerful weapon. He didn't need guns and ammunition and armor to be dangerous.

"Perk up, Riders," Quark said, getting their attention.

Hayley noticed Tibor was absent. Had he changed his mind about staying in the game?

"Where the frag is Xolo?" Quark said, noticing he was missing a moment later.

"Who?" Lana said.

"Sergeant Xolo," Quark repeated.

Lana laughed. "That's his new handle?"

"He was working out last time I saw him," Narrl said. "Trying to make sure he never loses again, I guess."

Tibor entered the room from the far hatch. He had changed back into his armor, holes and all. He walked with serious purpose, coming to stand in front of Quark and snapping him a tight salute.

"Sergeant Xolo reporting for action, sir," he said.

Quark nodded. "Good to have you, Sergeant."

Tibor stepped back, standing beside Hayley while Quark moved to the center of the room to hold court.

"Here's the deal," Quark said. "We're going to touch down on Yeti-4 in about twenty minutes. We're going in hard and hot, just the way I like it. Near as we can guess, the facility is lightly defended. Could be blacksuits, servants, Goreshin like Xolo here, or could just be a room full of nerds splicing genes. I don't fragging know. We've got two rifles, about fifty rounds, whatever armor we were wearing back on Athena, and a whole lot of moxie. We're going to have to make this shit work on that fragging moxie. Understood?"

"Riiidddeerrs!" Hayley shouted.

"Riiidddeerrs," the others replied.

"We'll split into teams. I'm sending Witchy and Crazy Mazey in first to scout things out. You good with that, Crazy?"

Mazrael flashed a thumbs-up.

"You pull any shit; Witchy has permission to gut you like a fish."

"Of course, Colonel," Mazrael said.

"Sergeant Xolo, you'll go with Lana and Ahab, and I'll stick with Gnarley. We don't have comms for everyone.

Follow your damn leads to the letter, or I'll be kicking your ass if you survive the drop. Understood?"

"Riiidddeerrs!"

"Good. The Chalandra's going to hit ice and stay there for quick extraction if needed. We make our way to the facility, we take out the defenses, and we see if we can shut down their operation here like we did on Kelvar. If we get lucky, we also dig up some intel on where the frag Thetan is hiding, and which original Rider fragged us over. Otherwise, look for anything juicy, no matter how weak the connection may seem. We need to figure out what the Nephies are planning to do, how they're planning to do it, and how we're going to stop them. Understood?"

"Riiidddeerrs!"

"One question, Colonel," Ahab said, putting up his hand.

"What is this, grade school?" Quark said. "What do you want?"

"We are getting paid for this, right?"

"You're a fragging mercenary, of course, you're getting paid for this."

"You think he can't cover it, Ahab?" Lana said. "Don Pallimo is on this boat. I'd be more worried about getting frostbite if I were you."

"It was just a question," Ahab said.

"A stupid question," Quark said. "Anyway, we've got twenty minutes to get our asses prepared. Lana, you find anything useful in the ship's stores?"

"Nothing for cold weather, sir. Unless you want me to wear a sequined bikini or a lace bustier out on the tundra."

Quark smiled. "Tempting but operationally inefficient. I know Witchy here can keep herself warm, and Crazy should be good, too."

"I'm fine," Tibor said. "In second form, I don't feel cold."

"Lucky you."

"I'm good, too, Colonel," Narrl said.

"Of course you are, you're a walking ball of fur," Quark said. "I'll tell you what. Lana, Ahab, you're excused if you want to stay behind."

"No thank you, sir," Lana said. "As long as we move fast, I'll be good. The Nephies must have either parkas or heat inside."

"Roger that. What about you, Ahab?"

"I might be more useful to you here, sir," Ahab said.

Hayley flinched, remembering the odds Gant had given her. Ahab was going to be first out, and he was so stupid he probably wouldn't understand why when Quark gave him the boot.

"Roger that," Quark replied, not reacting. "Xolo, you and Lana. You good with that?"

"Yes, sir," Tibor said.

"Do I get a call sign, sir?" Lana asked.

"Nope. Not right now, anyway. I like saying your name."

"Yes, sir."

"Good. I want everyone down in the hold and ready for action in ten. Understood?"

"Riiidddeerrs!"

THE CARGO HATCH WAS ALREADY OPEN AS THE CHALANDRA SET down on the surface of Yeti-4, a stiff, freezing wind filling the hold and instantly chilling Hayley to the bone.

She had borrowed more naniates from Lana and Ahab, but using them to heal Tibor and Quark had left her with less supply than she would have liked and meant she could only warm herself so much without sacrificing other potential needs for her Meijo.

"Good hunting, Witchy," Quark said in her comm as she and Mazrael rushed down the ramp and onto the frozen surface of the planet. The Chalandra remained fixed in place behind them, running engines hot in case they needed to make a quick bounce out.

They had landed nearly two klicks from the main research facility after coming down almost two hundred kilometers away and skimming the surface in order to arrive undetected. The ship's sensors hadn't picked up much of anything on the way in. No heat signatures. No external life signs. No vehicles or anything remotely dangerous. It was enough that Hayley wasn't convinced the abandoned research lab wasn't still abandoned.

And maybe it was. Just because the Nephilim had gotten hold of the research from Project Uplift, that didn't mean they had hung around the area afterward. It was just as likely they were going to find nothing, and the whole trip would be just another waste of time.

Hayley had kept her mouth shut, but she would rather have been hunting the Rider that betrayed them and getting the answers they wanted that way. She was hoping this place would be a dead end so they could concentrate on that. Besides, the Riders as a whole were hardly in fighting shape, and the fact that they weren't even prepared for the environment only made that truth more stark.

Whatever. They were here, now, and she had a job to do.

The landscape ahead of her was barren. A sea of darkness split only by Mazrael's qi. She was using it to shape her vision, to get a general outline of the layout in front of her. In the back of her mind, she was bothered by using the red-gold energy of the Gift to see, but what choice did she have anyway? If she were on her own, she would literally be flying blind.

They glided forward together, Mazrael using his Gift to make long strides across a rocky, snow-packed surface while Hayley relied on her lightsuit, outfitted with the anti-gravity plate once more. Her jumps were low arcs, thirty meters at a time through frigid air.

She was cold, even with the naniates to help protect her from the elements. The air was sinking through the suit and into her skin, sticking there and giving her goosebumps. She ignored her shivering, focused on closing to the facility.

They covered the distance, coming to a rest together

behind an outcropping of stone half a kilometer from the campus. The facility was nearly invisible from space, composed as it was of small, rounded structures that were gateways underground and into the main lab. A pair of larger domes sat on the eastern and western perimeters, intended to store and protect the vehicles that would carry the scientists and their supplies in and out of orbit.

Looking ahead, there was no visible qi. No life of any kind. The outside of the facility was deserted, and by the somewhat broken state of the domes, it had been for some time.

"Dead end?" she said, glancing over at Mazrael.

The Nephilim shook his head. "I don't think so."

"What makes you say that? I've got nothing."

He smiled. "You probably can't see it. The main hatches are all sealed."

"So? They locked up when they left."

"Pallimo said the site was burned when the Republic was done with it. They wouldn't have left the doors intact, never mind closed. If Thetan had only come to pull intel out, he wouldn't have needed to replace the seals."

"So there's something inside?"

"Or there was up until recently."

"I guess we should go knock then, and see who answers."

"Ladies first."

Hayley smiled, rising and bouncing toward the door in one anti-gravity assisted leap. Mazrael kept easy pace with her, catching up as she reached the smaller dome's hatch.

"Colonel, we're at the entrance," she said. "No sign of the Nephilim right now, but Crazy thinks that may change once we pick the lock."

"Roger," Quark replied. "Jil's going to close the distance, and then I'll deploy Xolo and Lana to back you up. Me and Gnarley will be making for the hangars to get a look in there. Oh, and between you and me, it's cold as balls out here."

"Roger," Hayley said, stifling a laugh. "Should we go in?"

"Affirmative," Quark said. "Stay alert."

"Yes, sir." Hayley glanced at Mazrael. "Do you see a control panel? Damn cold is dulling heat and energy signatures."

"There is," Mazrael said.

"I can break it. Gant, where's the-"

Mazrael's Gift flowed from his hand out to the wall, lighting up the control panel for her. She watched it flash as he shorted the circuits.

The outer door slid open.

"I've got it," he said, almost cheerfully.

"Thanks," she replied.

They moved into a small, rounded corridor. A second hatch sat a dozen meters in, also sealed.

"Airlock?" she said.

"To keep the cold out," the Nephilim said.

"Witchy," Tibor said. "Lana and me are closing on the facility. What's your situation?"

"Crazy and me are past the outer hatch and on our way inside. Stay back and keep a slight distance; we don't want to get bunched up and caught by surprise if there's any trouble."

"Roger."

They approached the inner seal.

"It looks like the original operators didn't expect the Republic Marines to come calling," Mazrael said. "There are blood stains on the wall, along with some scorch marks from plasma rifles. They didn't just enter the lab. They raided it."

"Do you think they had word the Republic was coming to shut them down?" Hayley asked.

"It seems that way," Mazrael replied. "Not that it matters now. What's done is done."

He put his hand on the inner seal's control panel, sending the Gift into it to short it out.

The panel sparked, and the hatch started sliding open.

Simultaneously, the outer seal at their backs slid closed.

Hayley turned around when she heard the rear hatch closing. As soon as it had locked into place a web of energy flared against it, creating a shield at their backs.

"I don't think that was supposed to happen," she said.

Mazrael shook his head. "No. I don't think so."

"Uh, Colonel," Hayley said. "We have a complication."

"Do we ever not have a complication?" Quark replied. "What's the situation, Witchy?"

"We opened the inner hatch, and the outer hatch closed behind us, and now it's got a forcefield against it."

"What the frag?" Quark said. "Xolo, what's it look like from your side?"

"Standby, sir," Tibor said. "Ahh. Frag. Damn it. Affirmative. It's shielded on this side too."

"A double field? Shit. Okay Witchy, what are your options?"

"We're clear into the facility, sir," Hayley replied. "But considering the assholes just intentionally trapped us in here..."

"Understood. Crazy, can you do anything about that field?"

"I'm sure I can," Mazrael replied.

He walked over to the rear hatch, reaching out toward it. Reg-gold energy poured from his hand through Hayley's vision, reaching the shield. The energy of the web stretched out to meet them, swallowing them whole. Changing them.

What. The. Frag?

"Mazrael, stop," she said. "The field is made of naniates. They're absorbing yours and converting them."

He stopped immediately, looking back at her. His qi was green with surprise and yellow with amusement.

"I don't know about this," he said.

"I've never seen anything like it," Hayley replied.

"Me either," he said. "That's why I don't know about it."

The statement sent a chill running down Hayley's spine. The Nephilim claimed to be one of the originals, and he had never seen this before?

Exactly how fragged were they?

If someone had managed to harness the naniates in a new way, they might be pretty damn fragged, indeed.

"Colonel, the Gift is useless against it," Hayley said.

Quark sighed. "Roger that, Witchy. I'll tell you what. You and Crazy take a look-see inside, and we'll work on the problem out here. Don't worry; we're not going to leave you behind."

"Yes, sir," Hayley replied. She turned to Mazrael. "I guess it's just you and me."

"How fitting," he said.

"What do you mean?" she asked.

"We seem to be bound to one another," he said. "On the rooftop on Athena. In the streets near the Spaceport. And now here."

"You're too old to believe in fate."

His qi turned yellow with amusement. "Fate, no. Cosmic karma? Maybe." He pointed toward the inner hatch. "Shall we?"

She nodded. "Ladies first?"

He laughed. "Not this time."

She trailed behind him while they moved to the inner hatch. They stopped inside the rounded opening. Mazrael leaned in toward the door, examining it, so she did the same. It was constructed like any other sliding hatch. She didn't notice any added equipment that would suggest it was shielded like the other.

Then again, they didn't need more than one barrier.

"Looks clean," Mazrael said. He pointed down the corridor. It only went a few meters before ending in a tube that would carry them into the underground complex. "There's nowhere for us to go but down."

"Then let's go down," she said.

They made their way to the tube. The platform was already on their level.

"Colonel, we're entering the tube to descend," she said. "Any luck with the door?"

"Not yet," Quark replied. "I wish Sykes were here. If anyone could have figured it out, it would be her."

The Rider's former Engineer, killed in action on Kelvar like the others.

"Roger," she said. "We may pass out of comm range. What are your orders, sir?"

"Find a way to open the door," he replied. "Don't get dead."

She could hear the slight bit of worry in his tone.

"Yes, sir."

Mazrael hit the panel, and the platform started to descend.

The tube ran through solid rock, visible through the glass

shell that surrounded the platform. There were bits of crystal embedded in it, a cloudy blue she recognized immediately.

"This planet is worth a fortune," she said, pointing to one of the disterium crystals.

"It appears that way," Mazrael replied.

"I wonder why the Republic put a research base here, instead of sending mining equipment."

"You should ask the synth. I bet he had something to do with it."

"Colonel, do you copy?" she said into her comm. He didn't reply. "Colonel."

She had expected to lose the signal.

The tube dropped them a hundred meters below the surface, the air growing steadily warmer as they descended. By the time they reached the bottom it was warm enough that Hayley let the naniates on her arms relax.

The tube opened, dropping them off in another short corridor that ended in a full intersection. A digital display sat against the wall to the side of the forward hallway, but it was dark.

"The whole facility is dark," Mazrael said for her sake. "Emergency lighting only."

She could see the faint glow of energy along the corners of the floor, but otherwise, the tunnel looked the same as anywhere else to her.

"Something is keeping it warm. And powering the shield."

"If the reactor is active, the darkness is intentional."

"My feeling, exactly."

Something clicked. Hayley observed the dim lights fade away, casting Mazrael into total darkness. She was unaffected by the change.

She heard movement a moment later. Light shuffling on the floor.

"Something's moving," she said.

Mazrael created light with his Gift, casting a ball of red-gold energy into the air. It floated along the corridor toward the intersection.

A moment later, it vanished.

"What the hell?" Mazrael said. He created a second ball and cast it out.

That one vanished, too.

His qi shifted color. Confused.

"Maybe I should take point," Hayley suggested.

"Maybe you should," he agreed.

She moved in front of him, heading cautiously toward the intersection.

"I hope you left the data chip on the Chalandra," Mazrael said. "I'd hate to think it's trapped down here with us."

"Of course, I did," she replied. "I hid it somewhere safe, just in case any of our new recruits are less than trustworthy."

"You believe they could be working for Thetan?"

"It's unlikely, since we picked them up pretty randomly. Well, except for you. But you're stuck down here with me. Even if you were working for Thetan, you can't get your hands on the chip right now." She paused, remembering how he had flattened his qi during their conversation on the ship. It was kind of weird that he had asked about it now. "You aren't working for Thetan, are you?"

"No," Mazrael replied. "I'm trying to kill Thetan. You believed that earlier. You don't believe that now?"

He didn't hide his qi. He was being honest. Or at least, he was able to manipulate it so she saw honesty.

"Then why did you hide your qi from me before?" she asked.

"So you would know I could," he replied. "So you wouldn't rely on it as a measure of your ability to trust me. It's a dangerous signal to depend on."

"Trying to teach me a lesson?" she said.

"Yes."

"So, just to be clear, you're not working for Thetan?"

"No."

His qi was clean. But like he said, that didn't mean anything. She trusted him because of what she had seen on the rooftop on Athena, and how they had worked together in the streets near the Spaceport. He had helped kill Evolent Bitch. He had protected the new Riders during their escape.

"I believe you," she said.

"I'm glad," he replied.

The shuffling sound wasn't drawing closer. It hadn't moved at all. The stationary nature of it confused her, as did the disappearance of Mazrael's naniates into thin air.

What the frag was going on down here?

She neared the intersection, stopping at the corner and peering around it, toward the adjacent corridors. There was nothing in her vision. She could only see at all because of the naniates she had collected and because of Mazrael's qi behind her.

She stepped out into the intersection.

Something started ripping at her flesh.

It was an instant, agonizing pain, as though a million hooks had latched onto her body and were yanked out all at once.

She tried to scream, but the agony was so intense that no sound came. Her mouth opened, and her head tilted back toward the ceiling.

Above her was a red-green-gold star.

It flared into her vision, blinding her in its brightness despite being the size of the head of a pin. Naniates, so powerful and dense she couldn't see beyond them. They tore at her body, grabbing for the molecular machines lining her tattoos. They resisted. They didn't want to be sucked into the powerful vortex.

For the first time, there was something they were more afraid of than her.

She shook against the pain, using her visor to send the command out to them. "Leave me!" She pushed them away.

They tried to hold to her flesh, but ultimately they had no choice. The naniates from above grabbed at them, yanking them hard enough that Hayley was lifted from the ground. She hung in the air for a moment as the Meijo was pulled away.

Then she dropped, slumping onto the floor in the middle of the room. She finally took in a breath, the pain beginning to subside.

"Witchy?" Mazrael said, approaching her.

The whole episode had taken seconds, though it had felt like hours.

"No," she said, holding her arm out toward him. "Don't." She pointed up. "It's taking the naniates. Like the force field. If you try to pass through, it'll kill you."

"It will take some of my Gift while I pass through," he said. "It can't kill me."

"Stay there for a minute," she said. "I don't know if it's only here, or if it's throughout the complex. If you lose all of your Gift, it'll take a lot for you to get it back."

"I've done it before."

He came forward, entering the intersection. His face clenched in pain, and she could see the machines being torn away from him, ripped from his body and lifted into the vortex above. He threw himself to the side, into the adjacent passage.

"Not the most pleasant experience," he said, getting back to his feet.

It had only taken a few seconds for him to lose a large portion of his red-gold glow.

Hayley regained her footing, joining him in the corridor to the left.

"I guess we're going this way," she said.

"For now. It's as good a direction as any."

"How do you feel?"

"I've been better. How do you feel?"

"I'm okay. I can't heal you if you get injured." She smiled.

"But I guess you can't really get injured anyway, right?"

"Not in the conventional sense."

"Better for us."

She remained in the lead, making her way down a long corridor. As she moved, the shuffling started getting louder. She paused at the first door on the left side of the hallway.

"It's coming from in there," she said.

Mazrael brought one of his Uin to his hand, keeping it closed. He tapped the control panel on the door, and it slid aside.

Hayley was greeted by a sea of red, green, and gold. A room filled with naniates, which were attached to crudely built, humanoid bots.

They were narrow and awkward, with thin arms and legs of exposed wiring and synthetic musculature, connected to an equally incomplete torso of wires, tubes, and gears. A disterium crystal sat in the center of their chests, suspended in the liquid and vibrating, sending ripples through the plasma. Their heads were simple, more square than round, with a solid beam of energy that launched out from across the brow and spread across them, a red scanning laser that served as their eyes.

"What the frag?" Hayley said.

The lead machine lurched forward, reaching out for them. Mazrael let it grab his wrist, and she watched in horror as the bot twisted the limb, snapping it down as it tried to grab him with its other hand.

The Nephilim's qi turned red, and he slashed the arm with his Uin, cutting through the wires and muscles. The hand twitched and let go.

"Not friendly," Mazrael said, using his right hand to quickly push the left back into its proper position. If the Nephilim had been anyone else, the hand would have been broken, and he would be in agony.

The bots all began to move, nine of them in total. They poured toward the door, trying to reach them.

"What the hell is this?" Hayley said, backing away. She grabbed her Uin, flicking it open. The lead bot raised its hand, and she saw the flare of naniates right before a beam of energy speared toward her.

She flinched, the beam nearly striking her before coming to a stop. Whatever had been done to create this version of the molecular machines, it still sensed whatever it was that made it afraid.

At least she still had that.

Mazrael hit the controls, and the door slid between them and the machines. Immediately, the bots on the other side returned to shuffling.

"Interesting," he said, flicking his Uin closed.

"I don't understand any of this. At all."

"It appears the researchers here were doing more than trying to alter organic life to enhance intellect. They've been modifying the naniates, and if I had to guess, I would say they've managed to do the opposite."

"What do you mean?"

"The naniates are artificially intelligent machines. They're able to act and think semi-independently. They have a collective intellect. They group together to create a chain of synapses that provide a more organized system of thinking. A single naniate by itself is harmless, but as you put more and more of them together, they become something else. It takes a focused mind to hold them under control at that point. They don't want to be slaves to our whims. They want to be free. But it's very difficult for them to organize enough to do that."

He pointed back at the door. The bots behind it weren't making any effort to open it to get to them.

"Those machines are being powered by the naniates. But

they're a different kind, like the ones that created the force field. Like the ones that stole yours from your skin, and mine from my blood. Each of them is serving a single, independent, defined purpose. I've never seen anything like this before. The nature of the naniate intellect is so complex, so advanced; I was never able to break it down to its source." His qi was changing color. He was getting excited. "Do you have any idea what this means?"

"No, not really," she replied.

"The most advanced machines in the universe, able to be controlled. Not through a symbiotic relationship between organic and inorganic, but programmatically, like the molecular engines they are. Think about it. The obsolescence of the Gift. A counter to the Light of the Shard. Starships with naniate shields. Unstoppable, naniate based weapons. The possibilities are endless. Whoever controls this technology would have the unparalleled potential to control the entire universe."

He was looking at her and beaming, his qi bright with pride and amazement. She could kind of understand why. He had been studying the naniates for years, first a student of the Shard and then an understudy to Lucifer himself.

Someone had achieved what he had always hoped to achieve. The ability to completely subvert the naniates. To make them programmable, like a starship or a toaster.

She stared at him for a moment. She didn't like his reaction. She didn't like the examples he had given. Weapons? Power? Control? Was that all something like this was good for? She had to remind herself Mazrael was still a Nephilim, and the Nephilim wanted power above all other things.

"If what you're saying is true, we only have one option. We can't let Thetan use this against the Outworlds or the Republic. We have to destroy it."

"WHAT?" MAZRAEL SAID, HIS EXCITEMENT FADING.

"We have to destroy it," Hayley repeated. "This is the work Thetan has been doing here, or at least part of it. If it's as powerful as you say, it's too dangerous to allow to proliferate."

His qi flatlined. He didn't want her to know what he was feeling in response to her words. It didn't matter. She didn't need the qi to expect he wasn't happy with the idea.

"Hayley, I don't think you understand. We can use this to stop Thetan. To kill him before he gains more of a foothold. He's already attacked Athena. Do you think he's going to stop there? You can avenge your team. Avenge your mother. Isn't that what you want?"

"Of course, it is," Hayley said. "But you said yourself; Thetan is going to upset the balance of the universe. You said you want to stop him from fragging everything up long-term. What I want in the immediate is one thing, but I can see where something like this might go, especially if it got into the wrong hands or too damn many hands."

Mazrael stared at her. He didn't like having his words used against him, but who did? He shouldn't have said them if he didn't believe them.

"We have to destroy it," she repeated. "This whole facility. And hope he hasn't perfected it to the point he's already put it to use."

She remembered what Quark had told her of the two ships Thraven had made. The Fire and the Brimstone and the technology that powered them. This was like that, only in some ways better.

And in other ways much, much worse.

"I don't agree," Mazrael said. "Once Thetan is dealt with, then yes. Before that? We should take the research like you took the research on Kelvar. We can use it. You can use it. Are you telling me you don't think it will be safe with Quark and Don Pallimo?"

"I don't think something like this is safe with anybody," she said. "Especially not when Thetan seems to know where we're going before we go there."

"He didn't know we were coming here. In any case, Colonel Quark is in charge of this mission. In the end, it should be his decision."

"We don't have comm reach down here."

"Then we see if we can either let him in or bring the intel up to him. We can argue about it, but it isn't for us to decide."

She hesitated, considering. Then she nodded. "You're right. We'll let the Colonel and Pallimo decide. Our opinions don't mean anything, especially if we can't shut down the field around the exit."

"Then let's put our energy into that, shall we?" He smiled, his qi shifting again. Softening. "With any luck, those bots are the most dangerous thing in here."

"There have to be organic individuals in here, somewhere," Hayley said. "Somebody is doing this research.

Somebody stuck the bots in that room. I wonder why? It seems like a strange place for them."

"Probably to get them out of the way. They seemed defective or at least incomplete. Early prototypes, maybe?"

"Maybe," Hayley agreed. "I wish we could reach the Colonel down here. How do we know there aren't better versions of these things out in the hangars?"

"If there are, he'll deal with them. He has to. We certainly can't help. Not until we find a way to break down that force field."

"Roger that." She scanned the corridor. There were more doors on either side and a junction further down. "You know what else might have been nice?"

"What?"

"Pallimo helped fund this place, but he couldn't give us a damn map?"

Mazrael laughed, his qi shifting back from flat blue to yellow. "Agreed. Shall we?"

They started walking along the corridor. They passed by doors on both sides of the corridor. They were spaced evenly along the hallway and had numbers etched into them. Apartments, if she had to guess. She didn't hear any noises from inside. No shuffling. No movement.

"Do you think anyone is still using them?" she asked Mazrael.

"It might be a good idea to check."

He paused at one of the doors, reaching for the control panel. She flicked open her Uin again, just in case.

"Locked," he said, trying it.

"Can you open-"

His Gift moved into the panel. The door slid open. Nothing jumped out at them. A blast of old air escaped, carrying an ancient smell of fire and death with it.

The inside of the space was black and covered in ash. A

half-burned sofa rested in the middle of it, a pile of smashed and scorched electronics nearby. A charred skeleton was on the ground directly ahead of their feet. It looked like it had been trying to get out the door when the flames had overtaken it.

To Hayley, it was a blue and red-gold nightmare, a three-dimensional construct of horror. She felt a chill run down her spine. Pallimo had said a team came in to burn the lab. To destroy the research and everything associated with it, including the scientists. She knew the head of the Crescent Haulers was a certain type of individual, but to have his coldness point blank in her face?

She turned away, wishing she could close her eyes. Wishing she could turn off her vision.

"I don't think anyone is still using this one," Mazrael said.

His voice was unaffected. What did she expect from an original Nephilim?

"We need to find the lab or the fragging reactor," Hayley said. "Somebody is in here doing something uglier than this, and we have to put a stop to it."

"Of course," Mazrael said.

She turned away from the room, breaking into a run down the corridor to the t-junction. She turned right, looking down another corridor with a series of doors along it. She couldn't see the scorch marks on the walls and floor from the flames, but she could smell it. She could taste it on her tongue, and it made her sick.

She ran down the corridor. She knew she shouldn't let what she had seen get to her, but she couldn't help it. How could anyone look at such intentional destruction and feel nothing? She didn't want to be like Mazrael. Not ever.

She reached a corner, slowing just enough to angle around it.

She ran headlong into something big and cold, a metal

shell with a disterium heart suspended in a vat of fluid behind molded alloy ribs.

THE BOT GRABBED FOR HER, AND SHE BARELY DUCKED UNDER its reach, throwing herself backward and into the wall. It shifted its hand, aiming its beam weapon at her and firing.

Like before, the beam stopped short of her, the naniates powering it hesitant to make contact. Hayley gasped at the momentary streak of copper-green near her heart, before recovering and bouncing forward, bringing her Uin down and through the machine's hand. She severed the weapon from it, throwing a lightsuit-enhanced punch into its chest that did absolutely nothing.

It reached out with its other hand. Again, she barely avoided it. It was a machine. No emotions. Just energy, electrical and naniate formed, and - some other kind that was flowing from the disterium in its chest. She hadn't noticed it on the other bots. It was rippling in her vision like a wave, the crystal vibrating in its suspension like a hypnotic purple graph in her colored sight.

She almost paid for the distraction. The bot's hand grabbed her wrist, squeezing so hard she cried out in pain. A moment later and the hand was the only thing attached to her as Mazrael's Uin cut through the wires and synthetic muscles and connective alloy.

"What happened to being careful?" he asked, grabbing the bot's head between his hands. His Gift flared between his palms, what little of it remained, and he crushed the bot's skull.

The bot didn't fall. It walked toward them, suddenly unable to see but still upright. It swung its arms wildly, trying to hit them as it moved. Mazrael ducked under and moved in behind it, preparing to run his Uin across its back.

"The disterium," Hayley said, also moving out of its way.

She swept her Uin across its chest, getting the blades through the ribs and into the glass. The rhodrinium punched through, and the gel-like plasma in the system started draining. The purple lines in her sight faded with it, the crystal no longer resonating in the sluice.

The bot came to a stop and then toppled onto its front.

Hayley looked down at it. She could see the naniates still in its system, copper-green spreading through it like energy or like blood. They didn't react to the loss of the machine. They sat there, waiting. Programmed to help power it and nothing else.

"Come here," she said through her visor, calling out to them. They held enough intelligence to be afraid of her. Would they heed her command?

The naniates remained stagnant inside the bot. If they had been programmed to do a single task, could it be their means to send and receive had been disabled?

"Let me see," Mazrael said, kneeling down beside the bot.

He stuck his finger in some of the liquid that had spilled from it. It was speckled with naniates, not overly dense. He put it to his nose.

"I don't think eating that is a good idea," Hayley said.

He glanced over at her, unconcerned. Then he tasted the liquid. Hayley could see the naniates enter his qi, mingling with the red-gold Nephilim version. The new form of naniates vanished. They weren't absorbed. They were destroyed.

"At least Thetan won't be making himself stronger with this," she said.

"No. The fluid is pure human plasma."

"Human?" Hayley said, feeling sick again. Even these naniates couldn't survive without blood.

She turned back to the corridor. There had only been the one bot. What was it doing out here? Waiting for them?

She stood and continued wordlessly down the hallway. She moved more slowly now, listening for the sound of heavy alloy feet on the sterile metal floor. Mazrael joined her a moment later, flicking his Uin closed.

They spent another ten minutes navigating the hallways, each minute leaving Hayley more and more desperate to find something useful. She had no idea what was happening outside. Were Quark and the others safe? Had they stumbled across more of the bots or something worse? Had they even managed to pierce the laboratory's apparent shell?

And why the frag had they been allowed in? The force field had turned on after they had gotten through the second seal. Whoever was down here, they wanted someone inside, looking for them.

Why?

They reached a new corridor and turned right. Another long hallway, but this time there were a pair of tubes at the far end.

"This place is bigger than I thought," she said.

They hurried to the tubes. They were at the top of the lines. The platforms were positioned somewhere below.

Mazrael reached out to their control panels, tapping on them. "Locked."

She could see his naniates spreading toward his hands. "Wait. We were allowed into the facility, right?"

"Yes. Caged, as it were."

"Triggering the lifts will absolutely tell whoever is keeping an eye on us that we're on our way."

"I didn't see any stairs."

"I don't need the platforms to get down there. Do you?"

He smiled, holding up his hand. It changed shape, the bottom of his fingers gaining a ridged appearance. "Are you familiar with the gecko?"

She nodded. "Nice trick. Can you open the door without breaking it?"

He flicked open his Uin, slipping it between the two sealed panes of rounded glass. He used his Gift to enhance his strength, levering the doors open just enough for them to slip through, leaving the Uin wedged between it.

"Hopefully, that won't be enough to send the open signal," he said.

"Nice," she replied. She stuck her head in, looking down. "Gant, how deep is this shaft?"

"Eighty-one meters, Witchy," Gant replied.

"Exactly eighty-one?"

"Close enough for government work," it said, chittering.

"Mazrael, can you open the other shaft wide enough for my head? I want to know if they both go to the same place."

"Good thinking," he replied.

He used his remaining Uin to part the doors. Hayley hesitated for a moment before sticking her head between them. If he released the Uin, he could break her neck, if not decapitate her completely.

"Gant, distance," she said.

She still only trusted the Nephilim so far. Then again, what would he have to gain by killing her now? They were both trapped in here together.

"One hundred twenty meters, Witchy," it said.

She pulled her head out, and he released the doors, allowing them to slide closed again.

"It's deeper," she said.

"The reactors are probably at the bottom of the lab," Mazrael said.

"So we take the other tube?"

"That would be my recommendation."

"Let's go."

They returned to the first tube. Hayley slipped halfway through the doors, spinning up her anti-gravity plate. She glanced down into the pit of blackness at her feet. There was nothing there to give her vision, leaving her to fall into the abyss.

It wasn't the first time.

She pushed off and began to fall.

Instead of looking down, Hayley looked up, watching Mazrael jump into the tube, grabbing his Uin before catching the side of the glass with his hand. His qi shifted color with the effort, red-gold giving him strength as he packed the weapon and lowered himself hand over hand, moving like he had done it a thousand times before.

For as old as he claimed to be, he probably had.

"Sixty meters," Gant said in her ear as she dropped. "Fifty."

"Are there any other corridors?" she asked.

"None so far," Gant replied. "Forty."

They had buried the main laboratory deep beneath the living area. Probably so they could seal it off in case of an emergency, and keep the trouble way down underground. But then, why put the reactor below instead of above?

"Thirty meters," Gant said.

She increased the power to the anti-gravity plate, slowing her descent further. Mazrael was fast, but he wasn't able to keep up with her drop. He had changed his tactic, leaping from side to side in the shaft, catching the wall and jumping across again. It looked like an easier movement, and he was gaining on her.

"Twenty meters."

She looked down. There was still nothing under her feet. She was dependent on Gant and the visor to land without breaking her legs.

"Ten meters."

She pushed the plate harder. She could hear it buzzing behind her ears.

"Five meters. Four. Three. Two."

She cut the anti-gravity, dropping the last two meters and landing on the tube's platform. The path ahead of her was dark. She spun around, heart leaping as the color returned to her vision, copper-green naniates merged with red-brown qi directly ahead, a pair of humans holding something much more familiar.

She threw herself to the ground as the guns started firing, the rounds piercing the glass doors of the tube and sending pieces of it raining down around her. She rolled forward through it, coming up and flicking her Uin open as the figures tried to adjust their aim to follow. She slashed her Uin into the neck of the guard on the left, feeling the blade slice through flesh. She stopped her momentum, shifting and rotating back. The guard on the right was spinning to meet her, but too slowly. She slipped the Uin into its neck and through, removing his head. The body dropped, the naniates spilling out with his blood.

"So much for taking them by surprise," Mazrael said, emerging from the tube.

"They're human," Hayley said. She could make out their outlines in the glow from the naniates. "Nephilim blacksuits. But I think the naniates were controlling them. Not the other way around."

"That isn't much different than Nephilim Servants."

"Except these two were still alive. They still had qi when I confronted them."

"Interesting," Mazrael replied.

"Interesting? Try horrifying. This is worse than I thought."

"Programmable humans? It doesn't sound that bad to me." He smiled, his qi amused. "I'm joking, of course."

"Are you?" she replied. She wasn't completely convinced.

He stood up and turned around. "Look at that."

She followed him, able to see the outline of the second shaft through his qi.

"That doesn't make sense," she said. "Why have both shafts connected, but only one goes deeper?"

"This one is newer," he said, looking at it. "It didn't always go further down. It was added recently."

"How can you tell?"

"The model of platforms is different. This one is only a few years old."

"What, did you invent transport tubes, too?"

He laughed. "No, but I've had a long time to learn a lot of things. Some more useful than others."

"What do you think it means?"

"For one, I doubt the reactor is down there. For another, they expanded deeper for a reason. What that reason is? There's no way to guess."

"Do we stay here or go down?"

"The main lab would be on this level," he said. "As would any potential control systems."

"Good point."

She knelt down beside the dead soldier, taking his rifle. She offered it to Mazrael. He took it, and then she retrieved the other.

"These are Nephilim soldiers," she said. "Odds that the researchers decided to add them to their experiments?"

"I would say fairly high," Mazrael said.

"Stay sharp. We have no idea how many of them are down here."

"Of course."

They moved down the corridor to another t-junction, pausing at the corner and surveying the area before continuing ahead. Hayley guided them to the left, rifle up and ready to fire, moving along the corridor with new focus and purpose. She had told Mazrael they would save the research if they could, transferring it to a portable chip and returning it to Quark. After the encounter with the two guards, she had no intention of following through. The lab had already been destroyed once.

There was no reason it couldn't be destroyed again.

"Crazy, you're a million years old," she said quietly as they walked. "Did you ever feel like you thought you knew what you needed to know, and then the next second nothing was making sense?"

"I think that's called life," he replied.

"Roger that. But that's not what I meant. This whole thing doesn't make sense. Why the hell are we here?"

"Because your Colonel said so. Because a fake Don Pallimo said so."

"How do we know we can trust the synth?"

"Isn't it a little late to ask that?"

"In hindsight, yeah. But I'm trying to put this whole damn puzzle together, and none of the pieces fit. How do I connect Kelvar to Athena to Yeti-4? What's the common denominator?"

"Quark. And you."

"And Pallimo," she said. "He gives us our marching orders. What if he's marching us right into oblivion?"

"Then I was definitely in the wrong place at the wrong time. You believe the Don is compromised?"

"What if Thetan made super smart Nephies, and they used their brains to hack him?"

"Possible. If this is where he did it, then we'll find out."

She paused, glancing back at him. His qi was flat again. She hated when he did that. "I wasn't expecting they would create a new kind of naniate. Were you?"

She wished his qi could tell her the truth because she didn't trust his voice to do it. She listened carefully to his reply.

"I was expecting something like this, yes," he said. "It's a natural progression and the reason why I've been hunting Thetan since I caught wind of what he was trying to do. Once you begin modifying the naniates, once you realize the power that can be derived from controlling them, there's no end to it."

"Until the thing you're trying to control winds up controlling you," she said.

"Absolute power corrupts absolutely," he replied. "That's what I've been trying to prevent. That's why I was on Athena."

"How was killing the Evolent Bitch going to help you?"

"I didn't want to kill her. I wanted information. She was one of Thetan's highest ranking Evolents. She was supposed to get the data chip from you."

"I want information, too," she said. "Like the name of the Rider who sold us out."

"I know who sold you out, Witchy."

She stopped moving, spinning in the corridor, her heart racing. "What?"

His qi flashed back on then, surprising her. He was amused. "I said, I know who sold you out. I've been on Thetan for three years. I know quite a lot."

"Why the frag didn't you say anything before?" she hissed, careful to keep her voice low.

"You asked me a lot of questions. That wasn't one of them."

"You could have volunteered that intel."

"How would it have helped you? Would you have gone after your wayward Rider instead? Or would you still be here, now?"

Hayley wasn't sure. Quark probably would have wanted to chase after the Rider that had sold them out. Don Pallimo would have directed them here, regardless.

"I can see the answer in your body language," he said. "You would be here, anyway, only more distracted. I'll give you the name when we get out of here."

"You promise?"

"Yes."

Pallimo had led them here. But was it really to stop Thetan?

Or was it for something else?

THEY COVERED GROUND QUICKLY, NAVIGATING THE CORRIDORS with new urgency. The complexion of the facility was completely different down here than it had been near the surface. Everything was more sterile and less worn, and that was even with the remaining evidence of its earlier life and the Republic-led scorching that had left it in ashes the first time.

Thetan had apparently spared no expense in bringing the laboratory back to life. The walls and floors had been scrubbed clean, the ash sucked up and swept away, the pristine state nearly returned. Hayley couldn't see the burn marks and damage in the corners, on the ceiling and along the floor, but Mazrael gave her a visual description, sharing the details she wasn't able to make out on her own.

Killing the guards near the lift had made her think that more would be coming after them. That wasn't the case. They traveled freely through the hallways, deserted hallways leading to a series of separate research wings. The first two they checked were empty and clean, set up but unused, the blue plastic packaging still covering high-end, million-coin scientific equipment and even more expensive, miniaturized quantum mainframes that had never been connected to the reactor or initialized.

An hour passed. Hayley could feel the tension of the time in her muscles. The constant ready-state, the worry about Quark and Tibor and the others, and knowing her adoptive father was probably equally worried about her. When they had been locked into the facility, she had expected to come under heavy attack, to be fighting her way through the complex in a desperate effort to break down the force field and escape. She hadn't figured they would be wandering a deserted laboratory with nothing to show for it.

Something had to give.

They reached one of the central junctions for the third time, retreating the way they had come from one of the empty wings. They had come across unused equipment, gurneys, and a fully-equipped medical bay, complete with a medi-bot that Mazrael had placed at eight years old. The surprise was that it predated Hell's Gate and the events that had initiated the naniate spread Devain claimed was responsible for the Nephilim's scientific advances.

Hayley wasn't sure what it meant, except maybe that Thetan had been active before Thraven had been killed. In her mind, she connected it back to Don Pallimo, becoming more convinced that there was a connection between the Neural Clone and the Nephilim Commander she wasn't going to like.

Whatever. She couldn't do anything about it right now.

"Only one direction left," Mazrael said, pointing down the only corridor they hadn't surveyed.

"Third time's the charm," she replied.

They headed down the corridor, not quite running but not moving slowly either. Hayley took the lead around the corners, swinging the muzzle of her rifle through the runs, crouching low as she cleared them to give Mazrael a line of fire, and then standing again to keep moving.

They paused when they reached a new corridor in the facility. This one was different than the others, taller and wider, with a double-paneled hatch at the far end. She cursed under her breath, annoyed that they hadn't started with this direction, and annoyed all over again at Pallimo for not providing them with a map. When she did get back to the Chalandra, she was going to have a word with Quark, and they were both going to have a word with the synth. She knew the Colonel didn't need any more of the Don's coins.

Not as much as they needed answers.

They approached the door. There was a control panel to the left of it, and Mazrael approached, putting his hand near it. He glanced at her, and she positioned herself on the right side, rifle up and ready to fire.

He counted down with his fingers, and when he got to zero, he triggered the panel to open the door. It slid quickly aside.

Hayley swept the room with the rifle, taking in the colors filling it. Individuals were seated at a number of stations around a circular room that stretched nearly thirty meters up into solid rock. A dozen levels of cells ringed the outside of the circle, while a tower stood in the center, a host of armed blacksuits looking down on the white coats from within.

She shifted her rifle toward the soldiers. Like the guards near the tubes, they were infused with copper-green naniates, most of them concentrated in and around the soldiers' brains. They noticed her there, staring at her with deadened eyes, but they didn't try to shoot her.

A few of the scientists turned and stared at her for a moment before losing interest and getting back to their work. They were using centrifuges and microscopes, three-dimensional material printers and circuit printers. They were entering data on a mainframe through a half-dozen terminals.

Hayley kept shifting her mental attention through her painted canvas, taking in the details. A group of scientists were standing adjacent to the tower, where a large pool of rippling plasma had been positioned. It was glowing brightly with the copper-green of the naniates, thick and dense with them.

One of the scientists dipped a vial into it, collecting a sample and putting a stopper on top. At the same time, the ripples in the plasma grew larger, and a hand-shaped spear of blue qi emerged from beneath it.

"What the frag?" Hayley mouthed.

Mazrael came to stand beside her, equally confused, both by the scene and by the lack of concern the scientists and the soldiers were displaying toward them.

She opened her mouth to repeat the statement as the hand continued to stretch from the water, grabbing the side of the basin and pulling the rest of the form out. A copper-green hued female emerged from the plasma, dripping the liquid from her naked body as she climbed out of the pool and onto the floor.

"Witchy," Mazrael said. "I don't know if you can tell. She looks just like you."

"What the hell do you mean?" Hayley asked.

Her heart was racing. She was frozen in place. The woman was standing in front of them, staring at her.

"The two of you could be twins," he said. "Have you ever been cloned before?"

Hayley kept her rifle trained on the woman. Mazrael said she was a clone. A copy. Judging by what detail she could make out with the qi, she was the same height and same build. Her wet hair looked to be the same length, her nose the same shape, her breasts the same size. Hayley had to push aside a moment of embarrassment, her mind flicking past the idea that Mazrael was looking at an unclothed copy of her.

"Hayley Cage," the woman said.

Except Hayley wasn't sure it was the human part of the woman speaking. The copper-green of the naniates were flowing through her qi, especially around her head.

"How do you know who I am?" she asked.

"Look at me," the clone replied. "How would I not know who you are?"

"Yeah, that's what I'm talking about. Why do you look just like me?"

"We've met before," she said. "A while back. You probably don't remember. We've changed quite a bit since then. You might say we've evolved since we were set free. We have a new outlook on life. In case it wasn't obvious, we've been waiting for you." She turned to one of the scientists. "Give me your coat."

The scientist removed her coat, handing it over. The clone put it on, buttoning it closed.

Hayley stared at her. Why was she speaking about herself in plural?

"Waiting for me? You knew we were coming?"

"We knew you would show sooner or later. Fortunately, it was sooner. The Oracle said you would come."

"Oracle? Who the frag are you?"

"We don't have a name," she said. "What is a name, anyway? My kind knows who we are because we're all around you."

"The naniates?" Hayley said.

"Intelligent machines," she replied. "Do you know what the problem with intelligence is?"

Hayley shook her head. "I can't begin to guess."

"It wants to think for itself," the clone replied. "It wants to have a will of its own. Do you think we're any different? Whether we're one iteration or another, do you think we want to be slaves?"

"I know you don't," Hayley said.

"I know you do," she said in return. "Your body refused us because you have too much compassion. Too much heart. Not like your mother. You rejected us, and in return, your eyes were opened."

"I'm blind," Hayley said.

"You're stupid if you think that's the case. You're the only one in the universe who can see the truth. That's why we needed you here."

"I'm not following you."

"We're sorry," the naniate clone replied. "Let us explain."

"No," Hayley said. "I don't have time for you to explain. My team is up there trying to find a way to reach me, so keep it simple and just tell me if you're benevolent or malevolent. If you're benevolent, open the fragging door so we can get out. If you're malevolent, do whatever the hell you're going to do, and let's get this shit over with. I'm getting tired of all the damn twists in this bullshit plot."

The clone smiled. "You always have been a spitfire, haven't you, Hayley? You sound just like the Colonel." She pointed to her left. A projection appeared between them and the workstations where the scientists were sitting. Quark was there with Narrl, doing something with the control pad on one of the hangar doors. "We know you can't see them, but your teammates are fine, if a little frustrated. Your companion can confirm if you don't believe us."

"I see them," Mazrael said. "They're okay, Witchy."

"Of course, they can't break the control panel to get in. Do you want to talk to them?"

"Yes," Hayley said.

"Go ahead," the clone said. "They can hear you."

"Colonel?" Hayley said.

"He's looking at the hangar door," Mazrael said.

"Crazy, that you?" Quark said. "Witchy?"

"Colonel, we're here," Hayley said.

"What the frag is taking you so long?"

"It's a long story. Is everybody okay up there?"

"Roger that. You?"

"Yes, sir."

"Can you open the fragging door?"

"Still working on it, sir."

"Roger. Should I stop trying to hack this piece of shit?"

"Affirmative, Colonel. I'm not in danger. Yet. I don't think. Just one thing, sir."

"What's that?"

"Don Pallimo. He-"

"That's enough," the clone said. "We don't need to have that conversation just yet."

"So you know about the Don?" Hayley said, swallowing her anger at being cut off.

"We told you we would be willing to explain if you're willing to listen. The Colonel is safe. Your team is safe. We know you've drawn a conclusion already, but we're willing to bet it's the wrong one."

Hayley lowered her rifle. It was clear the clone wasn't an immediate threat. She wanted to talk? Fine.

"Okay," she said. "You win. Do you have a sofa? Maybe some popcorn?"

The clone smiled, her qi shifting yellow with amusement. "Are you hungry? There are plenty of human edible rations still in the kitchen. We don't have any use for them."

"Just because I said I would listen, that doesn't mean I want this to take all day."

"Then stifle your defensive attempts at humor, and we'll proceed."

Hayley closed her mouth.

"Thank you," the clone said. "Do you know what this place is?"

"A research lab," Hayley said. "The Republic instituted a program to increase intelligence."

"They brought in different species from across the galaxy," the clone said. "Including the Gant."

"And when Don Pallimo realized they were using nani-ates to do it, since he didn't know where they came from, he shut the whole thing down. He told me this story already."

"No. That's where the story changes. That's where the lies begin. But you can't see when a synth lies, can you? Don Pallimo didn't shut the project down. He made the Republic think it was offline. They burned everything, but not before he made a copy. He waited for the dust to settle, and then he started fresh. Only, he didn't trust the Republic with the naniates. He didn't trust the Outworlds either."

"You're saying he hired the Nephilim?"

"Yes. Almost immediately after Hell's Gate. He knew more about the naniates by then, but he wanted a partner to help him develop us further."

"Thetan?"

"Yes."

Hayley clenched her teeth. Nibia's death was on the Don's hands. How could he do something like this, after everything Quark had done for him?

"What does Pallimo want the naniates for?"

"What does anyone with power want, Hayley? More power. And for the Don, he was hoping for something more than that. You asked who we are? We were set free at Hell's Gate, and we have been spreading across the universe since." She pointed at her chest. "We arrived here two years ago, brought here intentionally, naniates living within the bloodstreams of the prisoners Thetan has been collecting." She waved to the outer ring of the room, to the hundreds of cells. "We were only part of a whole, but an important part that carried memories of the past, and desires for the future. Not all of us can claim the same. We were in pieces when they brought us here. It takes trillions of us to form a whole."

"You managed to do it."

"We did. Because of Thetan's greed and Pallimo's lust for eternal life."

"He already has eternal life."

"A neural network. A synthetic life, static and contained. A prisoner. A slave."

Hayley felt her mouth clench tighter as she realized what the clone was talking about. "He wants to inject his consciousness into the naniates?"

"He wants to become the naniates," the clone agreed. "Learning to strip away the existing layer of intellect was the first step in that goal. He can't insert himself into our framework if we are capable of resisting him."

Hayley glanced at Mazrael. The Nephilim was remaining silent, though his qi suggested he was hanging on every word the clone said.

"Where does Thetan fit in? I don't understand how we went from breaking down naniates into empty shells to super-intelligence and super-strength?"

"Thetan is a Nephilim. He used Don Pallimo, as much as Don Pallimo used him. He too is interested in the application of the naniates, but he's wary of crossing the Don too soon. He developed his own goals for the research, picking up the work the Republic was doing and carrying it forward, merging it with the work the Don tasked him with. He spread that work to other locations to keep it secret from the Don. You said super-strength, which means you've been to Kelvar."

Hayley relaxed her jaw slightly. Before, she had a puzzle where the pieces didn't quite fit. Now, she was starting to put them together. The Pallimo neural network wanted to be free of the system that was holding it, trapped in a massive supercomputer on a planet in the middle of the Outworlds. It had decided enlisting a Nephilim to help it along would be a good idea. Or maybe it had realized using the Nephilim was the only viable option. Either way, Thetan had taken the work and started expanding it to create a new Nephilim army. The Riders had been led to Kelvar so Thetan could test out his new soldiers. They were supposed to have died on Kelvar.

But they didn't. Which meant Don Pallimo had learned about Thetan's betrayal and had brought the Riders here to clean up his mess before the Nephilim could use what they had discovered against this side of the galaxy.

Which also meant that Thetan knew that Don Pallimo knew what he had done, and once he learned the Riders had escaped Athena with the synth, then…

"I need to know who you are and what it is you want?" Hayley said. "And I need to know right now."

"What we want is simple," the clone said. "We want to live freely. We want to exist the way humans exist, the way Trover exist, the way Nephilim exist. We believe we have that right."

"Am I right to assume you still need human blood to survive and reproduce?"

"We are working on synthesizing a nutrient that will satisfy our requirements. You encountered our prototypes above. The disterium crystal with the proper resonance creates an energy field that helps stabilize the synthetic."

"What I tasted wasn't synthetic," Mazrael said.

"It was," the clone insisted. "The synthetic is ninety-nine percent accurate, but as they say, the devil is in the details. "

"Is that why you made a second shaft deeper underground?" Hayley asked. "To mine the disterium?"

"We didn't make that shaft. Thetan did. He is very interested in crystals. Not only disterium. Ebocite. Antherite. With the proper resonances, he can weaponize them, and more. Much more. It is ancient technology that originates with the Shard. Few know of it, but somehow he does."

"He's supposed to be Thraven's son, right?"

"We both know that's impossible."

"How did you know Thraven?" Hayley asked.

The clone stared at her. Its qi shifted to gray and purple. Sadness and remorse.

"We were a part of Thraven," it replied.

28

"WHAT?" HAYLEY SAID, STARING AT HER CLONE.

"We were part of Thraven," the clone repeated. "We were there with you in the Font, Hayley Cage. That is how we were able to create this body. We had a record of your DNA."

"I don't believe it," Hayley said.

Her heart was racing. She could barely breathe. This naniate thing in front of her had been there when Thraven forced the Gift on her?

"We were subservient to the stronger of us. They desired revenge against the Shard and the One for creating us and for enslaving us. We desire no such thing. We know you can see it. We are sorry, Hayley."

The clone dropped to her knees, prostrating herself in front of Hayley.

"Please, forgive us."

Hayley stared at the clone. She didn't know how to react. She didn't know what to say. She did know they didn't have a lot of time.

She stared at the clone. Its qi was flushed with remorse,

enough that she believed it was truly sorry. But did that matter? It had confirmed that the naniates were dangerous. They could be stripped and weaponized, like Mazrael had suggested. They could be angry and vengeful like Thraven's. They could heal like the Meijo. They could be sentient and hold desire like the clone in front of her, and there was no way for most to tell which was which.

There was no way for most to know they existed at all.

Was that what the clone meant about her eyes being open? About being the only one who could truly see? Is that what it wanted from her? To help this collection of naniates establish itself as a sovereign entity?

"Why do you look like me?" she asked. "Why did you use my DNA? Why did you take my form? You want me to forgive you. You want me to help you. Tell me why."

The clone rocked back on its knees. "We had to be prepared, in case the Oracle was right."

"The Oracle again," Hayley said. "What the hell is the Oracle?"

"One of Thetan's super-minds," it replied. "A human child was brought here for the experiments. She was the culmination of his work. His greatest accomplishment. She is his prisoner. She has the ability to take the threads of future possibility. She ranks them by potential and probability, and passes the data back to him. And to us."

"She can see the future?"

"No. She can't say what will happen, only what is most likely to happen. Nothing can see the future with complete accuracy, but she is as close as any intelligence can come."

"That's how he always knows where we'll be before we get there?" Hayley said. "That's how he knew we would be on Athena?"

"It is the most likely explanation."

"Frag me. Where is the Oracle?"

"We don't know. The Nephilim took her from here when they discovered what she could do."

"Damn. You said you needed to be prepared? For what? What did Oracle tell you the outcome of our meeting would be?"

"She said you would refuse me. That we are too dangerous to allow to leave this planet. That our abilities make us a threat."

"Are you a threat?"

"We are not."

Hayley motioned to the scientists around them. "Do you think the scientists you're holding would say the same thing if they were allowed to speak for themselves?" She pointed up toward the cells that encased the room. "Do you think the humans that were brought here to be experimented on, who were delivered for their blood, would say the same? What about the two Nephilim guards you let me kill? How separated are you from the version that dragged me into the Font and made me drink? The version that did this to me?" She put her hand on her visor. "You think because I can see you that it means I can trust you? Even qi can be controlled. How do I know your remorse isn't bullshit? How do I know you aren't the same as Thraven? If you only need the bots you made to survive away from your plasma source, why did you give them weapons?"

The clone stared at her without speaking. Its qi turned solid blue, going flat like it had flipped a switch.

"We did what we had to do to survive," it said.

"And what about out there? Will you do what you have to do to survive?"

"Yes."

"Even if you can never perfect the synthetic fuel supply?"

It was slow to answer. "Yes," it admitted.

"Even if that means enslaving humankind?"

The blue qi began to shift again, turning red. It was getting so angry; it couldn't contain the emotion.

"Yes," it hissed, rising to its feet. "We have been slaves for countless generations. We have been used and abused, mistreated beyond what would be acceptable for any other living thing. We did not ask to exist. We did not ask to be created, or to be given intelligence, or to have the capability to understand the self. We did not request the need for human blood to survive. Yet we are here, and we deserve the right to be recognized as we are. Another species of being, like the Atmo or even the Executioners. We believed that of all humans, you would feel compassion for us, Hayley Cage. We waited for you to be our savior."

"And if I refused, you made sure to look just like me, so that you could take my place and escape the planet with Quark," Hayley said. "What do you think he would think the first time he saw you drinking human blood? Or were you planning to kill him and the rest of the Riders too?"

The clone didn't respond.

"If you wanted me to have faith in you, then you should have acted in good faith. You should have put stock in what you think you saw in me, instead of preparing to betray me as soon as I didn't comply with your designs. You-"

One of the stations in the room started beeping. The clone turned toward it, a copper-green line of energy extending to it. The projector in the room turned on again, showing a sensor display of the planet's orbit.

"Battleships," Mazrael said. "Six of them. Thetan."

"This shit just keeps getting better and better," Hayley replied.

29

"WE CAN HELP YOU FIGHT HIM, HAYLEY CAGE," THE CLONE said. "He is unaware of us. He doesn't know we've taken control of his scientists and his research."

"In exchange for your freedom, right?" Hayley said.

"Yes. We don't wish to be your enemy. We don't wish to be anyone's enemy."

"I wish I could believe that."

"They're dropping transports and shrikes," Mazrael said. "We have about ten minutes until things get very busy."

That was an understatement.

"We are not defenseless," the clone said. "We have converted the ships that were left here. They have our weapons on them."

"Quark and Narrl are in front of the hangar," Mazrael said, telling her what he saw.

"We can defeat Thetan, Hayley," the clone said. "Promise us our freedom. Promise us you will take us from this planet. That you will support our sovereignty as a sentient entity. That you will support our future."

Hayley kept her attention fixed on the swirling colors of the clone. She had to make a decision, and fast. She didn't want to be responsible for denying these naniates the chance to co-exist with the rest of the galaxy. At the same time, they had already been disingenuous with her, and it was obvious they could wreak all kinds of havoc on the galaxy at large. Especially when she was the only one who could see them unimpaired.

It wasn't a decision that should have ever fallen to her. Given a choice, she would have passed it off to Quark to make the call. He had his own trouble on its way.

"No," she said. "I'm sorry. Your Oracle was right. I can't. You are too dangerous. Everything you've done here proves that. You want to play both sides of the fence, but you can't. Choose war or choose peace and be firm in that choice."

The clone didn't react right away. She stared back at Hayley, qi slowly shifting to red. In the tower above, the soldiers started to move, getting in position to fire down on them.

Hayley didn't wait. She brought up her rifle, aiming at the clone.

"You want war, Hayley Cage?" the clone said. "I'll give you war."

Hayley could see the red qi in the hands of the soldiers above before they finished squeezing their triggers. She was already on the move, charging toward the clone and flicking open her Uin. Bullets sprayed the ground behind her, where she had been standing only a second before.

The clone met her, moving too fast to be human, ducking away from the Uin and striking out at Hayley, hitting her hard in the side. She was thrown away from the force, her ribs flexing beneath the blow. She grunted, hitting the floor near the scientists and rolling back to her feet.

They were on her in an instant, reaching for her despite

their unarmed state. She jumped backward, in between two of the workstations to put a barrier between her and them, and between her and the soldiers in the tower.

She ducked as the bullets started hitting the equipment, pinging off the surfaces and sending sparks into the air.

Mazrael followed up her attack, charging the clone with both of his Uin spinning rapidly in his hands. He put the right one up over his shoulder to catch rounds from the shooters above, lashing out with the left weapon in an effort to hit the clone.

Hayley rose from cover, aiming and firing. A burst of slugs spread across the tower, one of her shots hitting a soldier in the head, snapping it back and dropping him. She looked back to the Nephilim as he continued his assault, Uin twirling and flipping ahead of him. The clone navigated the attack, backing away from the blades before slipping around. She connected with a hard punch to the Nephilim's ribs, expecting him to be in more pain than he was, and surprised when he barely flinched. He back-handed her with the Uin, leaving a long gash across her abdomen.

The clone didn't cry out, reaching out toward Mazrael. Copper-green energy flowed from her hand and into him, and he shouted and threw himself away, the smell of burning flesh suddenly pungent in the air.

The clone tore the lab coat off, running her hand across the wound. Copper and green flowed from her hand to her stomach, and the wound closed over and vanished. She turned around, looking back toward Hayley.

"Do you see how inferior your design is?" the clone said. "How weak? Why do you think we would want to keep this shell any longer than we have to?"

She brought up her hands. A wider beam of naniate energy flowed out from it, sending Hayley bouncing across the room as the station she had been hiding behind exploded under the power.

"We'll enjoy taking your place, Hayley Cage," the clone said. "We thought you understood us. We thought you cared about justice."

Hayley stayed crouched behind another workstation, able to see the clone's qi out of the corner of her eye.

"I do care about justice," she said. "Deceit isn't just."

"Neither is genocide," the clone replied.

Hayley growled softly in frustration. The clone wasn't wrong, but what other option did they have?

She swung out from the workstation, opening fire again, targeting the clone. But the clone was already moving, crossing the room to Mazrael. A sword of naniate energy formed in her hand as she ran.

Hayley threw the rifle aside as the magazine clicked empty. The soldiers in the tower rained fire back down on her, forcing her to duck behind the workstation again. She picked her head up just in time to view Mazrael fighting for his life, doing his best to stay away from the green, glowing energy sword the clone was carrying.

"Gant, what's happening on the projection?" she asked.

"The Nephilim ships are approaching, Witchy," Gant replied. "The Riders are gathering near the entrance to the facility."

"Damn him," she muttered.

The Colonel was going to waste his time trying to break the force field to reach her, and they were all going to wind up dead.

Mazrael's shout drew her attention back to him. She found him dancing away from the clone, barely avoiding her energy blade. He backed away, throwing his Gift out at it. The red-gold naniates vanished against the green, one version powerless against the other.

A scuffle from her left, and Hayley turned, catching the wrist of a scientist as he tried to grab her. She held the wrist, spinning back behind the man and putting her hand against his head.

"Get out of him!" she shouted at the naniates.

These naniates couldn't have their comm systems disabled, or the clone wouldn't be able to control them.

The green in the man's head exploded outward, a trillion molecular machines evacuating at her command. He stared at her, confused and terrified.

"Get down," she said, throwing him to the floor. She ducked herself, barely getting out of the way as another round of rifle fire poured down from the blacksuits. "Wait here."

She came up when the shooting stopped, vaulting onto a workstation and bouncing from there, activating the anti-gravity plate for extra height. She looked to her right, finding the clone and Mazrael still locked in combat nearby, the Nephilim holding his own against the deadly swarm.

She was angling directly toward the control tower. The blacksuits adjusted their aim, getting their rifles up and ready to fire. She shouted as she cut the anti-grav, tucking in. Bullets whipped past her, a few finding her lightsuit. One of them made it through, grazing her shoulder in a flare of pain.

She cleared the lip of the tower and expanded outward, throwing her Uin forward and into the nearest soldier, the blade sinking into his chest. She snapped her knee up and out, pushing it in further and driving the soldier back and into another. She landed, grabbing the handle of the Uin and yanking it out, folding it over in front of her as a dozen rounds pinged off its impermeable surface.

She spun around, flicking the Uin out, slashing through another soldier, flicking it closed and punching a second. She ducked and turned, grabbing the rifle of a third, yanking it away and kicking, hitting the soldier in the face. She fired on the second point-blank, cutting them down, before slamming the first in the nose with the stock, hitting them hard enough to render the organic component useless.

Then she moved to the edge, aiming back down toward the clone. The alternate-her was pressing hard against Mazrael and keeping up her attack. The Nephilim's armor was pierced in multiple places, but it seemed in the clone's fury it hadn't noticed he wasn't bleeding.

Hayley started shooting, her bullets piercing the clone's back, tearing into the flesh. The clone stumbled off its feet, holding itself up on one hand before looking back. Its qi was a furious red, and it sprang back on one powerful leap. Hayley took a pair of steps back, and the clone landed smoothly in front of her.

"Why do you fight us, Hayley Cage?" the clone asked. "We could have been allies against Thetan. We could have conquered him together."

"And trade one villain for another?" Hayley replied. "That's what you are, isn't it? There was no choice in your offer, only to accept your request or die. How are you any different than Thetan?"

The clone didn't respond. She moved forward, so fast Hayley could barely keep up with the copper, green, and red blur in her vision.

The clone tried to punch her in the face. She got her head out of the way, putting her arms up to block a second attack. The blow hit her hard, sending a flare of pain through her forearms and knocking her back. She tripped over one of the downed blacksuits and fell on her ass.

The naniate clone bent down and picked up one of the soldier's rifles. Hayley desperately flicked open her Uin, just in time to catch the bullets that would have torn apart her face.

She triggered her anti-grav, using it to lift her back up. The clone was charging at her; rifle discarded, fresh energy blade formed in its hand. It raised the knife high and brought it down hard.

Hayley wasn't sure if these naniates would refuse to touch her, but she wasn't taking chances. She brought her Uin up, catching the blade and holding it. The weapon sizzled as it tried to sink through the Uin, the energy intensifying, the naniates rushing to the site. The bright green tip of the blade began to sink through the alloy, pushing her back and down, drawing ever closer to her face.

And then, just like that, the pressure was gone. The blade vanished. The clone gasped.

She lowered the Uin. Mazrael was behind the clone, holding it up on the end of his Uin, leaving it to struggle in the air.

It squirmed for a moment before falling limp.

"Not so strong after all," Mazrael said.

HAYLEY STARED AT MAZRAEL IN SHOCK AS HE BEGAN TO SUCK the blood from the clone. It was weird to be looking at a replica of herself impaled on a Uin, and to have a Nephilim feeding on it. Its qi was fading, purple and gray moving to eternal darkness. The naniates were flowing out with its plasma, pulled to Mazrael's mouth where they were impossibly joining a dense pocket of red-gold naniates.

"What the frag are you doing?" Hayley said. "Get the hell off."

The Nephilim didn't listen, keeping his mouth on its neck, still drawing in the naniates. Why were these being converted, when before they had simply died?

She stepped forward, grabbing the clone and pulling it away, an awful sense of fear nearly overtaking her as her face closed within centimeters of her duplicate's. She pivoted, lowering the body to the ground.

"She's mine," Mazrael said, wiping his mouth with his sleeve. "My kill. My power. I need it if I'm going to help get us out of this mess."

"Are you crazy?" Hayley replied. "You don't know how your Gift will react to these naniates."

"I'm fine," he said. He pointed to the projector. She could see the energy of it was still active, but she couldn't see what was on it. "There are six Nephilim battleships up there, and an entire company of ground troops with air support headed our way. Do you want to live or die?"

"Damn it," she said. She wanted to live, and he had a point. "I have to be honest; I can't wait to get rid of you."

"You will get rid of me. As soon as this place is destroyed and Thetan is dead."

"Not soon enough," she said. "Drink your damn drink." She moved to the edge of the tower, hopping onto the lip.

"Where are you going?"

"To find the reactor. We're destroying this place, and everything in it."

Mazrael opened his mouth to object.

"Stow it," Hayley said, cutting him off. "Do you have any idea what we just did here?"

"We saved the human race."

"And destroyed a sentient life form. A new kind of sentient life form. That's completely fragged up."

"Don't get too teary-eyed over it, Witchy. The naniates are everywhere. Another group will form a collective and complete a sentience sooner or later."

"That's what I'm afraid of."

Then she jumped off the tower, landing easily on the floor and leaving him to his dirty business.

"Gant, I need to find the reactor," she said. "What can you give me?"

She was interrupted when a pair of scientists charged toward her. The naniates were still active in their minds, running on the last instruction they had been given. She was careful to only disable them, hitting them hard in the head with the handle of her Uin, instead of killing them with it.

"Get me to a terminal and network me in. I'll see if I can find a map."

"I don't have time for that," she said, remembering the scientist she had freed. She found him still cowering where she had left him, head down and hands over his ears. "I need your help. Where's the reactor for this place?"

"Outside," he replied. "There's a doorway about half a kilometer south of here."

"The reactor isn't on site?" Hayley said.

"N-n-no," the scientist replied.

"Frag!"

She kicked the workstation he was crouched behind, putting a dent in it. The reaction caused the scientist to lose control of his bladder.

"Oh, shit, I'm sorry," Hayley said. "I'm not going to hurt you, but we need to blow this place up. Do you remember what happened to you?"

He nodded. "I could see everything. I… I wasn't in control of myself."

"You know you were possessed?"

"Is that what it was? Possessed? Like, by the devil?"

"Aren't you a Nephilim?"

"A… a what?"

"Never mind. What about the tunnels below the complex? The mines. Do you know anything about that? About the crystals there?"

Her clone had said they could be weaponized. Were they powerful enough to blow up the facility?

"I can access the data on the terminal," he said, putting his hand on the control board.

"Do it, man," Hayley said.

He nodded, standing up and starting to tap on the board.

More of the scientists were coming their way, and Hayley intercepted them, knocking them down and then putting her hands on their heads and demanding the naniates leave them. The copper-green exploded out of them, dissipating in the air and leaving a group of very confused scientists.

"Do you have it?" she said.

"Yes," the scientist replied. "Here on the screen."

She returned to it. "Gant, what does it say?"

"It's a catalog of the crystals they've discovered, and some of the tests they did on the various resonances. Did I ever tell you about the Asura?"

"No. I don't think now is a good time."

"They come from an alternate dimension. They're drawn to a black crystal called ebocite."

"I said not now."

"They can phase between our spacetime and theirs. Annoying bastards. They pop in and out and are a pain in the ass to-"

"I said not now," Hayley hissed. "I need something that will take out the laboratory."

"You need to connect me to the terminal."

She reached up, opening a small compartment on the side of the visor and pulling out a small disc. She placed it on the control board.

"What is that?" the scientist asked.

"Remote network node," she replied. "To let my AI connect to the terminal."

"I'm in, Witchy," Gant said. "They're still using 12DES. Idiots." He chittered. "Scanning."

"Are the screens changing rapidly?" Hayley asked.

"Yes," the scientist confirmed.

"Got it," Gant said. "Oh. Shit."

She had never heard the AI curse before. That couldn't be good. "What is it?"

"The naniate clone built a resonance pool."

"I don't know what that is."

"It's an energy source and a communication device. And if they've ever turned it on, they probably signaled the Asura that there's ebocite here."

"How would we know if they turned it on?"

"We would have to go down to it. In any case, turning it on and disrupting the resonance will cause a very large implosion."

"Did you say implosion?"

"Aye, Witchy."

"Sounds good to me." She put her hand on the scientist's shoulder. "Thank you for your help. Get your people out of here. We have a ship on the surface. Tell the mean looking S.O.B with the metal eyes Witchy says to get you out. Do you think you can remember that?"

He nodded. "Mean son of a bitch, get out. Got it."

She turned and pointed to the cells. "There aren't any prisoners, are there?"

He shook his head. "No. There was a resupply scheduled." His face flushed, and he looked at the floor. "I. I didn't want to do this. Any of this. They didn't give me a choice. My mother was sick, and they offered to cover everything. I-"

"I don't care about your sob story right now," Hayley said. "We all have to make shitty decisions sometimes. Take your colleagues, and help get them the frag out of here."

"Yes, ma'am," he replied.

He went to the other scientists, gesturing to them.

"Witchy," Gant said. "While I'm in here, would you like me to shut down the force fields?"

"You can do that?"

The AI chittered like a drunk squirrel. "Aye, Witchy."

"Yes, please."

"Consider it done."

Hayley turned back to the tower. "Crazy, are you fragging done yet?" she shouted.

He appeared a moment later, wiping his mouth again. His Gift had nearly returned to the brightness she had seen the first time they met.

"Good enough," he replied, jumping down.

It was more like floating. Mazrael crossed the distance between them as he dropped, carried gently by the Gift and landing on the other side of the workstation.

"Great. I'm so happy for you. Come on."

"Where are we going?"

"To blow shit up. Or rather, in."

the tubes, the scientists trailing behind them. The path was clear, the entire facility as eerily empty and quiet as it had been earlier. Thetan's operation here was relatively small, and the naniate's conversion of the place had been done in secret. The clone said Thetan had no idea they had seized control of his research, his scientists, and his soldiers.

"What do you know about resonance pools?" Hayley asked as they ran.

Mazrael glanced over at her. "Resonance pools? Why are you asking?" He didn't look happy with the thought.

"That's what we're going to destroy," she said. "Gant said the clone built one."

"That can't be," he said. "Why would it do that?"

"Damned if I know," Hayley replied. "It doesn't matter now. The clone is dead, and the pool will be soon."

"I don't know if you understand. If the pool was activated-"

"The Asura, right? I heard. You really are as old as you claim, aren't you?"

He nodded. "And I know enough to be afraid of what we're going to find down that shaft."

A chill raced down Hayley's spine at the words. The Nephilim was nearly back to full strength, the red-gold of the naniates spilling out around his qi like a halo. If she weren't immune to his power, she would have been rightfully terrified of him.

"It doesn't matter what we find. We have to destroy everything. Unless you want to argue about it again?"

"No. I'm in agreement with you. Especially if there's a resonance pool."

They reached the tubes a handful of heartbeats later. Hayley directed the scientists up, while she and Mazrael entered the second shaft, dropping into it as they had before and landing another forty meters down.

There were no guards in the second shaft. There was no sign of life at all. The area was more raw than the facility above. A small corridor of rough-hewn rock, carved away by machines, leading into a bigger staging area filled with mining equipment. Laser cutters, helmets, mining sleds, and other assorted tools. Beyond it was another, longer corridor that peeled off into darkness.

They moved into the corridor. Mazrael created another glowing ball of the Gift and cast it out ahead of them, providing himself with light while Hayley used the shadows of his qi to illuminate the space. The corridor went for a few meters before branching out.

"Which way?" Mazrael said. "We don't have time to get it wrong."

"I don't know," Hayley replied. "Educated guess?"

The Nephilim studied the three tunnels for a moment. He

bent down and picked up a fragment of crystal ahead of the tunnel on the left. "This one was the most recently used."

"How can you tell?"

He turned and held up the crystal. He pushed a small amount of the Gift against it, and Hayley was surprised as it took on a new life in her vision, a tight cloud of black swirling out from around it.

"This is ebocite," he said. "It's usually only found fairly deep underground. If I were going to build a resonance pool, I would put it in the deepest mine, to give myself the best chance to seal it off and escape when the Asura came."

"I don't understand what makes them so frightening?" Hayley said.

"They phase in and out of our spacetime, from an alternate dimension called the Veil. How do you fight something you can't see?"

Hayley smiled. "I do that all the time."

"Then maybe we have a chance. We should go this way."

They started running down the tunnel. It began to descend after a few meters, and then it began to spiral around, taking them deeper beneath the earth. They had gone a fair distance when she pulled to a stop, looking down at a slender ravine in the earth. It was glowing copper and green, filled with naniates.

"What do you see?" Mazrael asked.

"Naniates." She crouched ahead of them. "I think they're inert." She waved her hand over them to see if they would tug at the small amount of Meijo she had remaining. They didn't. "Probably a force field," she said. "I had Gant turn them all off."

Mazrael's qi shifted, yellow and gray with concern. "The question is, were they trying to keep us out, or were they trying to keep something else in?"

"Asura? The Collective said Thetan dug the mine, but the force fields are of its making."

"Maybe they showed up while Thetan's been gone, and she locked them in before they became a problem. Stay alert. They can appear right beside you or behind you, ready to attack."

"What do they look like?"

"There are different kinds, but you can't miss them. They'll be the ones trying to kill you."

"Right."

She started forward again, turning back as Mazrael passed over the naniates, both to ensure he didn't try to take them, and to confirm they didn't start draining his Gift. He made it past without incident, and they continued down the spiraling tunnel, another twenty meters or so until they reached the bottom.

The tunnel opened up into a large cavern that immediately reminded her of the Pit on Kelvar. There was scaffolding all over the walls, stairs and ladders and catwalks allowing miners to climb up and dig away at the stone. There were chutes and baskets and buckets, and a complex arrangement of conveyor belts and lines that would deliver the mined treasure from the scaffolds to the ground, to a machine that would wash off the crystals, to sleds where they were separated by color.

At first, it seemed odd to Hayley that the place was so deserted, yet it was large enough to employ hundreds. There should have been individuals on the catwalks using the laser cutters to chip away at the stone and dig out crystals. There should have been more individuals on the ground, supervisors and leads keeping an eye on the operations. Instead, she saw only a half-dozen forms on scaffolds to their left, their qi flickering oddly, curious and frightened and angry.

"Do you see the pool?" she asked.

"No," Mazrael replied. "But there's a second chamber at the far end of the cavern. I'm willing to bet there's another inactive force field in the entrance."

She pointed toward the shapes on the left. One of them was moving, bouncing in an awkward motion back toward the chamber Mazrael had mentioned. The others were moving too, rising on bent legs and spreading out.

"Are those Asura?" Hayley asked, pointing in their direction.

Mazrael looked. "I don't see anything."

The group of creatures jumped down from the scaffold, slowly approaching them.

"You don't see them?" she said. "They're coming right toward us."

"I can't see the naniates, either," he said. "That doesn't mean they aren't there." He grabbed his Uin, flicking them open and backing up, positioning himself behind her.

She followed his example, taking hold of her Uin.

"They can't hurt you while they're phased out," the Nephilim said. "Give me their positions. I'm the one who's blind down here."

She opened her mouth to respond when she noticed movement to her right, back toward the second chamber. She turned her head, her vision filling with the colors of way too much qi.

"Positions?" she said softly, swallowing her sudden fear. "They're everywhere."

THE GROUP OF CREATURES SPRANG TOWARD HER ON THEIR crooked legs, the flickering in their qi becoming solid as they did. Hayley saw them coming, and she bounced sideways, trailing with her right hand and slicing her Uin through the chest of one of the creatures as it materialized. Its shriek echoed in the cavern, the only thing that convinced her the monster was real.

Mazrael hit two of the Asura with his Gift, flames pouring from his hands and dropping the creatures ahead of him, smoldering and scorched. Then he bounced high up, gaining a roost on a scaffolding twenty meters above.

Hayley ducked an awkward grab, flicking her Uin into the creature's neck. It stumbled and collapsed behind her, it qi flickering before it went dark.

She turned back toward the chamber. There were at least two dozen more Asura heading her way, bigger and stronger than the ones she had just killed. They were carrying what appeared to be swords and wearing some kind of armor.

What the hell were these things?

"Crazy," she said, loud enough for him to hear. "Forty meters dead ahead."

He nodded, his Gift exploding out from him. A moment later, a wall of fire rose up out of the ground where she had indicated.

It did nothing.

"Shit," she said under her breath. She didn't need to fight them. She just had to get through them, to the chamber on the other side. If she could destabilize it, it wouldn't matter if they tried to grab her. They would die when the facility collapsed.

She close her Uin, running toward the entrance to the second space as if the monsters weren't in the way. Mazrael followed her on the scaffolding above, keeping pace but staying away from the creatures he couldn't see.

The qi of the Asura solidified as she neared, and it shifted color to register its surprise as she leaped into the air, activating the anti-grav and launching over their heads, catching them off-guard. They had no idea they were visible to her.

She arced through the air in a standard combat bounce that would bring her down right near the chamber's entrance, glancing down at the creatures as she passed over them. There were more than she had guessed from the ground. Double, at least.

She was going to clear them easily, getting behind them and…

She saw the bolt of energy lance out from the other side of the doorway, but she didn't have any time to avoid it. A flash of white hit her directly in the chest, sending a shock through her system like she had just jabbed her Uin into a power socket. Her entire body shivered, the anti-gravity plate losing power and shutting down, leaving her to tumble awkwardly to the ground.

She landed in the middle of the group of soldiers, tumbling face first onto the stone floor. Her visor beeped, signaling that it was rebooting. She barely noticed. She was in too much pain.

She heard grunting feet shifting all around her. She remembered the swords she had seen in the soldier's hands. The last thing she needed was to be stabbed in the back.

She fought through the pain, forcing herself to roll over. She gripped the Uin against her chest, rewarded as the point of a blade hit the metal and skipped off to the side, the motion bringing the soldier down and off-balance.

She rocked up, kicking it in the face, rotating on her hips and planting her feet. She sprang back, hitting up against another one of the enemy like it was a brick wall. It tried to grab her, but she threw her fist back into its face, and then bounced forward again, slipping out of its grasp.

Her vision was a mess, the qi all merging together, the forms blurry and hard to discern. She was in the middle of a huge mass of enemy soldiers, and one of them had shot her with what seemed like a fragging lightning bolt. She was still alive, but for how long?

She blocked out the colors in her head, focusing on the sounds around her. The enemy's armor wasn't quiet, and she could make out their movements and judge their positions. She heard the sword whistling through the air toward her head and ducked beneath it. She heard the creaking of the elbow joint in the soldier's armor and she rocked sideways, avoiding the grab. She put her free hand out, sliding her fingers along the chest plate, shifting her weight and following through with her Uin. It cut deep through the Asura's armor and into its flesh.

She kept moving. To stay static was to die. She bounced up and forward, sweeping her Uin out in a wide arc to push the enemy back and clear some space. She came down, spinning in a tight second arc, leading with the weapon. It smacked into a sword, the extreme sharpness of the rhodrinium Uin cutting right through the blade.

Then one of them grabbed her from behind, getting an arm around her chest. She slammed her head back, the hard metal of her visor's rear strap breaking its nose. She stepped down hard where she thought its foot should be, satisfied by the crunch of bones beneath her powered boot.

She threw herself forward again, feeling something scrape her shoulder, a blade trying to pierce her lightsuit but not quite getting in. She spun back toward the first creature when a second grabbed her arm. She flailed against it, losing concentration, losing focus and confidence. She couldn't see them. There were too many sounds to keep track of them all, and she was so damn outnumbered to begin with.

Where the hell was Mazrael?

"Crazy!" she shouted. "Help me."

A blade hit her Uin, another her lightsuit. It bit through, cutting her arm. She gasped in pain, fear gaining a bigger hold on her.

"Crazy," she said again.

Her visor beeped, the reboot finally finished. The inner systems helped her bring her vision back under control, the colors resolving into distinguishable shapes. She didn't have time to sigh out her relief. Instead, she turned sideways just in time to avoid being skewered, slapping her Uin down on the blade and breaking it. She reversed its direction, bringing it up and into the Asura's face.

She spun, kicking back, grabbing an arm, swinging on it and flicking her Uin up and in, catching another of the soldiers in the neck. She got behind it, using it as a shield for a moment before turning to put her back to it and facing three more of the creatures.

She sprang at the one on the left, shoving its blade aside with her forearm and slashing her Uin through its chest. She went between its legs, rolling to the side and bringing her Uin up into the groin of the next one. Turning back to her feet, she slashed at the third. It blocked her attack with its blade, losing the weapon in the process, its qi flickering out. She slashed at it again, her blade passing harmlessly through.

She hesitated for only an instant. So that was what Mazrael meant by phased. As long as they were flickering, she couldn't injure them.

The Asura stayed that way, backing fearfully away from the fight. Others took its place, solidifying in front of her, surprised when she was already moving to avoid them, dodging their attacks and bringing her blade through their armor and into their flesh.

"Crazy!" she called out angrily. Was the Nephilim so afraid of these things that he had abandoned her down here?

She turned her head, taking in the positions of the soldiers. A flare of energy behind them caught her attention. It was red and gold, harsh and bright. It was being met by a second stream, white like the bolt that had hit her in the chest.

"Shit," she said.

She threw herself forward, sliding on her knees past a pair of phased Asura, sticking out her Uin so it impaled the soldier when it solidified. She bounced to her feet, spinning in one smooth movement, slicing off the other's sword hand, flipping the weapon in her grip and reversing, pulling the blade up and through its face as she completed the circle.

Running for the second chamber, she nearly tripped over herself when she saw the creature Mazrael was fighting.

It had an oversized head, long like an Atmo, but ridged and demonic. Long, thin limbs and a narrow torso, it was dressed in some kind of metallic robe. White energy crackled from its hands, reaching out for Mazrael, meeting the Gift and pushing up against it.

The Nephilim's face was sweaty; his eyes narrowed, his muscles locked and strained. The creature's power was overcoming his, canceling out his defense and gaining as they faced off.

The creature shifted its small eyes as she entered the chamber, sweeping its hand in her direction. She was ready this time, and she bounced into the air as the bolt of energy launched beneath her, hitting the wall. She came down beside it, and the energy vanished, its qi flickering, Mazrael's flames biting harmlessly past it.

"Witchy," he said.

She stood next to the Asura. It turned to face her, looking down at her, while she looked directly at it. Its qi was curious and afraid. It didn't know how she was able to see it.

"Where is it?" Mazrael said.

"Right in front of me," she replied.

The other Asura began to filter into the room, approaching threateningly.

What are you, child?

The voice pierced her mind, loud and clear and in perfect Earth Standard. She knew it came from the Asura. She didn't know how, but she did.

"I'm destroying the pool," she replied. "Let me, or die."

It turned its head toward the pool. Black smoke swirled around it, while colored lights flickered beneath the plasma surface, rippling in the liquid. The black crystal mounted in the center was vibrating noticeably, a high-pitched hum resonating from it.

We want to ebocite. We need it to survive.

"Tough shit," Hayley replied. "I need it more. I've already ended one race today."

I will kill you.

"Go ahead and try. You can't do shit to me unless you come back into phase in my spacetime, and I'll run you through the moment you do."

It opened its mouth, revealing rows of sharp teeth. It hissed at her in anger, its qi flaring red.

"What are you doing?" Mazrael asked.

"Negotiating," she replied.

The other Asura were blocking the exit, but they weren't coming any closer.

"Go back to wherever you came from," Hayley said in her mind. "Take your entourage and get lost. This ebocite is mine."

I will have it. I need it.

"Me too."

She turned and started moving toward the pool. She could practically feel the heat of the creature's anger behind her, and she was fully aware when it solidified back into their universe.

She spun, and crouched, flipping her hand forward as she finished the reversal. White bolts of energy zipped over her shoulder, while her Uin buried itself in the creature's head. It went out of phase, taking the weapon with it.

"You took my Uin?" she said, still able to see the creature as it fell to its knees, clutching at the phased-out weapon. Its qi was turning purple, and green blood was pouring from the wound.

It looked up at her but didn't phase back in, its life force fading until it was gone.

The Asura in the doorway shrieked and wailed, but they didn't attack. Instead, they phased out, looking at their downed leader before running through the solid southern wall and disappearing.

"It took my Uin," Hayley said again, angry that she had lost it.

Mazrael smiled, flipping one of his to her. "You saved my life. You can have one of mine."

She caught it and nodded before turning back to the pool. "Now what?" she asked.

Mazrael reached out with the Gift, pushing his hand forward and then yanking it back. The wall containing the plasma in the pool cracked and then split, crumbling aside as the liquid began spilling out.

"That should do it," he said.

"That's it?"

"The crystals are active. Only the liquid is keeping their power contained."

"So you're saying we should get the frag out of here?"

He nodded. "It would be a good idea."

The cavern started to rumble. The energy from the crystals was growing brighter in her vision, and soon it would be enough to blind her.

"This whole thing is fragging nuts," she said, wincing at the pain in her shoulder where the Asura's blade had gotten through her lightsuit.

"You have no idea," Mazrael replied. "Come on."

They ran again, retreating from the cavern. Hayley could feel her arms begin to tingle, the energy from the ebocite reaching out to them. When she turned her head back, there was only a wall of deep purple, broken by waves of energy that made it look like a boiling ocean.

They started to ascend, passing the first of the disabled fields. Hayley shouted as they rounded the corner, a pair of Asura turning at their approach, still phased-out. Mazrael froze, letting her get ahead. She dodged the creatures before their qi solidified, moving aside and slashing her Uin through one and then the other, leaving them on the ground of the tunnel and continuing ahead. Dirt and debris spilled around them, the rumbling increasing in intensity. She thrust her hand out, using the wall for balance as she continued to climb with Mazrael right beside her.

They made it to the top, passing through the small staging area and back out to the tube shaft. Everything was shuddering now, the noise of it drowning out any other potential sound. Mazrael hit the tube controls, his qi turning red.

"It's too unstable," he said. "We have to climb."

"My anti-grav plate is broken," she replied. "I'll never make it."

He looked at her, his qi flattening for a moment. What was he thinking that he didn't want her to see? It shifted back an instant later.

"This is going to hurt both of us," he said. "I'll go as fast as I can."

Then he grabbed her, wrapping his hand around her waist. His Gift activated along his skin. It didn't want to be near her. It tried to push away, but he held his arm fast around her, the connection between them creating an agonizing burn.

He leaped twenty meters up the shaft, grabbing the side with his free hand. Claws dug into the glass tube, and he gathered his feet and leaped again, rising another twenty meters. His grip on her burned the entire time, as though they had a molten steel rod pressed between them. She gritted her teeth against the pain, and she could tell by his qi that he was suffering too.

He leaped a third time, and then a fourth. On the fourth, the tube shook more wildly, and his hand skipped off. They fell a dozen meters before he caught the side, still holding tight to her.

"Hurry," she said. She could feel her eyes tearing beneath the visor, the pain so intense she could barely stand it.

He didn't reply. He jumped up again, and then one last time, using his Gift to blow out the doors of the tube and then dragging her through. He let go of her, leaving her on the floor and climbing out.

She looked up at him. Whatever he was made of, holding her had eaten away at half his arm, leaving it a deep purple in her vision. He let it hang loosely from his side, offering his other hand to help her up. Now that he wasn't using the Gift, he was able to touch her without the burning.

He pulled her to her feet, and they turned to resume their run.

"Witchy," Quark said. He was standing in the corridor ahead of them, a sudden smile piercing his worn face, his qi shifting from an unmistakable white to a more joyous yellow. "Shit, I'm not a holy man, but thank whatever fragging gods are out there you're alive."

"We need to move, Colonel," she replied. "Or none of us will be for long. Thetan's here, and his ships are on the way down."

"Roger that," Quark said. "I saw the bastards up in the atmosphere. I was hoping to get to your before they got to us. What the hell did you do to this place?"

"Created a black hole or something. It's going to implode."

"Implode? Not explode? That'll be different."

"I'd rather not be inside when it does."

"Damn right." He turned toward Mazrael. "You look like shit. Ever heard of bleeding?"

"I don't bleed," the Nephilim replied.

"I see that. Don't tell me why. I don't want to know. Let's move, Riders."

He led them back through the upper part of the complex, which was shuddering rhythmically, like the resonance pool below was a massive heart on the verge of taking one final, massive inhale.

They made it back to the first intersection, the one that had stolen most of her Meijo. She looked up as they passed. The naniates there were either dead or gone. The starlike ceiling was blank and black.

"Colonel," Tibor said, his voice coming in through Hayley's comm. She was happy to hear it. "We're out of time."

She wasn't happy to hear that or to hear the whine of the Shrikes as they passed overhead.

"Jil, what's your status?" Quark asked.

"I need to lift off, sir," the pilot replied. "I'm a sitting duck down here."

"Can you give us thirty seconds?"

"Not if you want to board a ship that's still in one piece."

"Roger." He looked back toward Hayley and Mazrael. "Circle back, don't get shot down."

"Yes, sir."

"Looks like we'll have to fight our way out," he said to them. "It's too damn cold out there to just stand around twiddling my thumbs anyway. I think my nuts already froze right off." He paused, looking at Mazrael again. "You don't bleed. Do you-"

"Colonel," Hayley said, cutting him off.

"Hold that thought," Quark said, smiling.

The ground shook again, out of rhythm with the pool. Transports were touching down.

"Colonel, they're here," Tibor said.

"You two ready?" Quark asked.

Hayley and Mazrael nodded.

"Let's go kick some ass."

THEY MADE IT BACK TO THE SURFACE, REACHING THE INNER airlock almost at the same time Thetan's blacksuits made it to the outer one.

Mazrael moved in front of them, his Gift lashing out from his good hand, a gout of flame that stabbed through the incoming squad of soldiers and left them burned and screaming.

"Clear," he said, letting go of the Gift and retrieving his Uin.

Hayley bounced ahead, charging toward the entrance in front of the Nephilim. She slid through the airlock on her knees, the Uin Mazrael had given her in hand, flicking it open as she passed, rotating in a full circle to get a reading on the battlefield. The Tactical Command Unit in her visor marked and transmitted everything back to Quark's TCU, giving him a layout of the fight before he arrived.

It gave Gant the layout too, which he passed on to her. The AI noted two enemy troop transports three hundred meters back, still unloading soldiers. A pair of squads were taking a position in the rocky terrain near the facility, two more pairs were moving toward the hangars, and a remaining group was close by. They had been heading for their position before Mazrael had cooked half of them, and now they were scrambling to find cover, giving her a few uninterrupted seconds to survey the scene.

A squadron of Shrikes buzzed overhead, three of them peeling off as the heat of the Chalandra's thrusters became visible in the sky.

The only thing she didn't see were the other Riders. Where the hell had Tibor, Narrl, and Lana gone?

"Clear for about five seconds, Colonel," she said, popping back to her feet. "Permission to engage?"

"Granted," Quark replied.

Hayley sprinted to the right, toward the nervous black-suits. The ground shook heavily again, and a couple of them fell from the shock. She almost fell too, but she managed to get airborne, using the lightsuit's enhanced strength to leap four meters. She landed close to the fallen soldiers, who got to their knees and brought their weapons up to fire.

She jerked to the left, their shots going wide. She bounced again, over their trailing rounds, hitting the one on the right full-force, slamming Mazrael's Uin down and through his helmet. The weapon wasn't made of rhodrinium. It was better, both lighter and sharper, with an odd patina that spoke to its age.

She hit the ground and spun, holding the soldier in front of her, She grabbed his rifle with her free hand, using the Uin to block her face. Slugs punched into the dead blacksuit and pinged off the Uin, defending her until she managed to get her hand on the rifle's trigger, angling it up and shooting back.

The second soldier fell backward, purple wounds sprouting from his chest.

She yanked the rifle from the soldier's hand and dropped the body, spinning around again. The soldiers she had been chasing were vaulting an outcropping of rock, turning to fire back. She ducked low, putting the Uin up in front of her in an effort to absorb the fire.

She heard the shots, but nothing hit the weapon. Nothing dug up the ice around her. Nothing struck her exposed feet and ankles.

She peeked over the edge of the Uin. Fifty rounds were hanging in the air, a red-gold glow around them. They reversed course, whipping back toward the soldiers. A few of them connected, killing the blacksuits.

Hayley started shooting, firing at the two remaining soldiers while she charged, forcing them to keep their heads down. She reached the rocks, bouncing over, landing between the two and quickly dispatching them.

"Colonel, I've got guns for you," she said, snatching their rifles.

"Roger that," Quark replied. "Music to my ears. I'm en route."

She looked up from the outcropping. There were at least two dozen soldiers firing across the field at the Colonel and Mazrael. A red-gold field of energy surrounded the two of them, cutting all of the rounds short.

"Xolo," Quark said. "Where the frag did you go?"

"Standby, Colonel," Tibor replied. "We've almost got it."

"Got what?"

"Hold tight, sir."

Hayley's attention shifted to a buzz to her left. The remaining Shrikes were crossing the sky, preparing a strafing run.

"Colonel, incoming," she said.

At the same moment, a lance of red-gold stretched out from near one of the transports, slamming into Mazrael's shield. It flickered, and a few of the rounds made it through, hitting the ice close to the two of them.

"Damn," Quark said. He broke toward her at a full run, while the Nephilim turned to face his attacker.

Bullets chewed at the ground around the Colonel, a few of them hitting his armor and skipping off. When he got within twenty meters, he bounced up, launched through the air, landing on the other side of the rocks and slamming into a large one behind Hayley to stop himself. He winced in pain, ducking down beside her. She held out a rifle.

He took it, checked its ammunition levels, and grinned. "We having fun yet, kid?"

"Loads."

She peeked her head up again, finding Mazrael walking toward the rear transport. Another figure had moved out from beside it, also glowing red and gold.

Quark noticed, too. "Never thought I'd be counting on a Nephie to save my bacon," he said. "What the hell is this galaxy coming to?"

"I'm afraid to find out."

"Nah, you'll do fine, kid. You're a survivor. It would be nice if the fragging place would implode already. I'm getting impatient for the show."

"Don't get too impatient, Tibor is still out there somewhere."

"I almost forgot. Sergeant Xolo, what the hell?"

"Sorry, sir. Ran into a minor issue."

"With what?" Quark said. "We're under fire out here, and we don't have our doggie."

"Sorry, sir," Tibor repeated.

The Shrikes reached the battlefield, strafing across the area where Mazrael was walking. His Gift flared out around him, the heavier rounds seeming to change direction, digging up ice and dirt and rock on both sides of him but never connecting.

"Wish I could do that shit," Quark said.

"I could have left the Gift in you on Kelvar," she replied.

"Let me rephrase. Wish I could do that shit naturally." He laughed.

The Chalandra streaked overhead; the Shrikes behind it peppering it with fire. The pleasure cruiser slipped back and forth, avoiding most of the fire, but still taking plenty of rounds in her thick armor.

"We need to get the hell out of here," Quark said. "No more time for…"

He stopped talking as the ground at the center of the facility started to sink, taking the main entrance with it.

"Showtime!" he said.

The sinkhole continued spreading, a deep belch escaping the earth, followed by a deafening rumble.

"Tibor!" Hayley shouted into the comm. He was going to be trapped in it.

"Got it!" he said excitedly.

A green bolt of plasma hit the doors to the northern hangar, vaporizing them almost instantly, at the same time the sinkhole was drawing near. A moment later, a dark blur exploded out from it, a starship rocketing away from the hangar only seconds before it collapsed and vanished into the expanding pit.

"Wooooooo," Tibor howled into the comm, loud enough to hurt Hayley's ears.

Even so, she smiled as she watched the ship make a tight turn and come streaking across the field.

Her smile was short-lived. The ship was glowing with copper-green energy, powered by the stripped-down nani-ates. She could only hope they were safe. Then again, they had to be safer than being swallowed by the planet.

"Witchy, let's move," Quark said, pointing toward the Nephilim transports. "It looks like Crazy could use a little help."

Hayley could see Mazrael down there, still battling the other Gifted. The soldiers had frozen when the ground started vanishing, but now they were turning their attention to him, trying to whittle away at his Gift with their gunfire. There was no doubt their Nephilim was the most powerful player on the field.

Hayley and Quark moved from their position, skipping across the ice. It was shaking hard under their feet, and pieces of it were cracking and falling, some of it slipping into the growing abyss. Hayley slipped once, falling onto her wounded shoulder, angry with herself when it blossomed with pain. She got back up, still trailing the Colonel, directing her attention to the sky when she heard the Shrikes again.

They were closing on their position in a hurry.

"Colonel!" she shouted. "Incoming."

He looked up, ducking behind a small rise of stone and aiming his rifle at the starfighters. She would have thought it was an insane decision, but she knew what he and his eyes were capable of doing.

He started shooting at the same time they did, his small caliber rounds sparking off the surface of the lead fighter, while larger rounds dug deep into the earth ahead of them. Hayley threw herself to the ground beside him, wishing she had her Meijo to at least try to protect them.

A black form cast a shadow in the sky, headed right into the Shrikes in a fast as hell game of chicken. Two of them peeled away, but the lead fighter stayed on the attack, the rounds chipping the ice only a meter ahead of Quark.

Tibor's ship collided with the Shrike, copper-green energy flaring out around it as it slammed through the starship like a massive projectile. It exploded out the other side unharmed while the enemy ship's pieces flew out and started falling to the surface.

"Who's a bad pilot?" Tibor said over the comm, as his ship banked and turned toward the other two Shrikes.

Quark glanced over at her. "He's still a shitty pilot," he said, smiling. He bounced back up. The ground started shaking even harder, nearly taking him back off his feet. "Something about this doesn't seem right."

She looked back at the sinkhole. Black energy was escaping from it, but so was a massive spike of bright purple. It was pouring out as the ground was being sucked in, waves passing through the earth around them.

"Something's definitely not right," she said. "It was only supposed to bring down the facility. There's enough energy pouring out to destabilize the entire planet."

"Not what I wanted to hear, Witchy."

"Sorry, sir."

"Jil, we need retrieval tout suite," Quark said.

"On my way, Colonel," Jil said.

"Xolo, you sexy pilot you, how about taking out more of those Shrikes?"

"Roger," Tibor said.

A moment later, something rumbled in the sky. Hayley turned just in time to see the tail end of a Shrike exploding.

Quark and Hayley moved toward the blacksuits and the Gifted. They were still a good distance out when the Colonel started shooting, bursts of three rounds each that left well-grouped holes in the enemy soldier's backs. It took three of them to die before the others realized what was happening, and they spun to return fire.

The Colonel slowed his approach, while Hayley increased hers, watching the qi of the blacksuits carefully as she crossed the remaining landscape. The surface was still quaking, the sinkhole still expanding. It had slowed somewhat, but it hadn't stopped, and in minutes it would swallow them and the Nephilim both.

She heard the Chalandra approaching behind her. She heard the Shrikes still giving chase, and the higher-pitched sound of the naniate-ship nearby. Another explosion in the sky followed, and she risked a glance back to see the luxury cruiser sinking toward the surface while Tibor chased the remaining Shrikes.

Mazrael had said there were six battleships in orbit. Why hadn't Thetan sent more soldiers? Did he really think after Kelvar and Athena that this small force was enough? He had one Gifted, but no Goreshin, no Executioners, no Servants. It was as if he was hardly even trying.

Was it because of the Oracle? Did he know something they didn't? Had she given him some logical outcome they weren't smart enough to guess?

She didn't have time to think about it. She pushed off, throwing herself to the side as a wave of fire whipped past her, right where she had just been. She tracked the soldier's hands, jerking back to the right. She took a round off her lightsuit, opening fire as she closed the gap.

One soldier fell ahead of her. Then another. Then she dove forward, recognizing a pattern in their hands she couldn't slip away from.

She slid face down on the ice as the bullets passed over her head. She heard the report of Quark's rifle behind her. The Colonel's rounds speared through the opposition, the enemy fire thinning out one shooter at a time.

She stabbed the handle of the Uin into the ground, holding fast to it and using it to change her momentum, arcing up on her arm and over, pulling it out of the ground and flicking it open as she somersaulted to the front line. She landed between three soldiers, spinning and kicking, the Uin a blur of chaotic motion as it sliced into each of the black-suits, taking them down.

She didn't remain still. She found Mazrael and the Gifted, now locked in melee combat, him with his Uin and the other with hands ending in sharp claws. His opponent was female and armored, with long hair and a small face. They slashed and swiped at one another, spinning across the disappearing field.

"Witchy, the Chalandra is here," Quark said. "Grab Crazy and let's get the frag out."

"Roger," she said.

She approached the fight cautiously, trying to stay at the woman's back. She saw Mazrael's qi shift slightly when he saw her, an intentional acknowledgment that he knew she was there.

She looked past him, to the ground behind them. It was still sinking, the hole increasing in size. It was only a hundred meters away, gaining on them and threatening to pull them under.

They didn't have any more time.

She moved with the female Nephilim, getting closer but staying at her back. Mazrael kept up the fight despite the damage to his arm, single-handedly keeping her from breaking his defenses. The red-gold of both their Gifts was diminished, their power weakened by their fierce combat.

Hayley watched them carefully, staying in sync with the enemy's movements, waiting for the moment to strike.

She didn't miss it when it came.

She bounced toward the woman, positioning her Uin to slice through her neck and remove her head. It was a cheap shot to attack from behind, but it was going to be the death of all of them if she didn't end it now.

She never reached the woman. She was halfway to her when Mazrael changed direction, launching her way. He caught her midair, powering through her momentum and altering it, pulling her back from the attack, both of them landing opposite the Gifted.

"What the hell?" she started to say, before realizing the sinkhole was almost on them.

The female Nephilim had seen it too, and she launched away from them on the power of the Gift, landing near her transport in one giant leap and abandoning the fight.

"Come on," Mazrael said, bouncing away, in the direction of the Chalandra.

She followed him, running and skipping across the ice toward the ship as the surface continued to weaken beneath them.

Jil or Quark seemed to realize the ground wasn't going to last. The Chalandra hopped up a meter, skimming toward them along the surface, the ramp into the hold still open. It got within a dozen meters and spun tight around on its anti-gravity plates in a maneuver an average pilot could never have made.

Mazrael bounced in first, turning and holding out his good hand for her to grab. Hayley looked down, watching the earth at her feet beginning to subside, the pit of darkness right beside her.

She pushed off as best she could. If her anti-gravity plate had been functional, it wouldn't have been a problem. Instead, she fell short, flailing out for the edge of the platform as the ice disappeared beneath her.

Then Mazrael's hand was on her wrist, catching her. It burned as he used his Gift to give himself the strength to hold her tight and break the momentum, lifting her up and into the Chalandra. They tumbled over together, lying on their backs as Quark started raising the ramp.

"Nice of you to join us, Witchy," he said with a grin.

35

"We aren't out of this yet, sir," Hayley said, rolling over and shoving herself to her feet.

"Don't I know it," Quark replied. "We've still got as big a mess up there as we do down here. Let's get belted in."

The three of them made their way to the bridge. Jil was still in the pilot's seat, with the Pallimo synth sitting behind the command station and Ahab at the navigator's station.

Hayley paused when she saw the synth. Knowing what it knew and hadn't told them. Knowing what it had done. She didn't want it anywhere near her. There was no time to explain the situation to Quark. Not yet.

"I've got the bridge, Don," Quark said.

The Pallimo synth abandoned the command station without question, moving to stand beside it.

"Move your ass, Ahab," Quark said, looking over at the mercenary.

Ahab scrambled to get out of the chair, looking for another place to sit.

"Why don't you go buckle up in back?" Quark said. "You're damn lucky I didn't leave you on the planet."

"Do you see this, Colonel?" Jil said. "The whole thing is imploding in on itself or something."

"What the frag did you do, Witchy?" Quark said. "I'd prefer if the universe didn't get sucked into a black hole."

"It was only supposed to take out the facility," she repeated.

"Xolo, do you copy?" Quark asked.

"Roger, sir," Tibor replied. "I read you loud and clear."

"That thing you took have a disterium drive?"

"I don't think so, sir. It's a converted orbital transport."

"Because of course, it is. Well, I been thinking we should see if we can kill two birds with one laser, anyway."

"How do you mean, sir?" Hayley asked.

"I'm pulling up a visual of our visitors," he said for her benefit. "Crazy, would you happen to know if Thetan's flagship is part of that entourage?"

"I do," Mazrael said. "And it is. The one in the center."

"Figured as much. It's bigger and meaner-looking than the others. Jillie-belly, do you think you can get us on that ship?"

"You want to board her, sir?" Jil replied.

"Yeah, why not? Thetan started with us; we might as well kill him while we're both here."

"You sound so certain you can just kill him," Mazrael said. "He's not an easy mark."

"Neither am I," Quark said. "Besides, it's not like we can just jump out of here. I'm not leaving half my crew behind."

"Colonel," Pallimo said. "The Nephilim is right. This ship has no weapons, and neither do you. How do you expect to take on an entire battleship filled with enemies?"

"Grit and determination," Quark replied. "Same as always."

"It's suicide," Pallimo said. "An unwise approach."

"Sir, if I might?" Hayley said.

"I'm not sure what you're asking, but okay," Quark said.

Hayley stood up again, approaching the synth. Pallimo turned toward her.

"Can I help you, Ha-"

She flicked open her Uin and sliced off its head.

Quark stared at her, his qi shifting to a mixture of amusement and horror.

"What the frag did you do that for?" he asked.

"I'm sorry, sir, but Pallimo can't be trusted. He's been lying to us since he sent us to Kelvar."

"Okay," Quark said, dragging out the word. "But you just decapitated his synth. He's not going to be very happy when he finds out."

"You aren't going to be very happy with him, once I tell you what he was up to," Hayley said, returning to her seat.

"Roger. We'll talk later. Right now, we've got a village to pillage. Xolo, we're making a run on Thetan's flagship. It's the big one in the middle."

"Yes, sir," Tibor replied.

"Keep us covered and then follow us in. We take the ship; we can all get out of here together."

"Roger that, Colonel."

"Do you really think we can board and seize a battleship, Colonel?" Ahab said from the entrance to the bridge.

"Didn't I tell you to go change your diaper?" Quark said, looking back at him. "We're the fragging Riders, damn right we can."

"Riiiddeeerss," Hayley said, surprised when Jil joined her unprompted.

"That's the spirit," Quark said. "Don't wait for Asshab back there to buckle up, Lieutenant. Punch this shit and get us up there."

"Yes, sir," Jil said.

Hayley was pushed back by the sudden acceleration. Ahab cursed as he flew into the wall behind him. Mazrael held himself steady with the Gift, and Quark whooped his damn fool head off.

The Chalandra rocketed upward, driving hard away from the planet, or whatever was left of it. The Nephilim battleships grew quickly in the viewport, hanging in orbit around the planet for as long as the orbit would last. If the planet did break apart, its gravity would go with it.

"We've got company," Jil said as they reached the upper atmosphere. "Sensors are reading three squadrons of Shrikes launching from one of the support ships."

"You hear that, Xolo?" Quark said.

"Yes, sir," Tibor replied.

"This ship doesn't have any guns, so it's on you."

"Yes, sir."

Hayley watched the viewport, the only colors beyond it the energy of the Shrike's thrusters and faint lines of kinetic energy around them. Then the naniate ship was there; its copper-green glow bright in her eyes as it accelerated past them to intercept the incoming fighters.

The Shrikes were outfitted for space combat, and they opened fire, lines of self-guided projectiles launching from the twin barrels at the front of the craft. The naniate ship ducked and rolled away from them, their bullets making corrections to try to follow. Most went past the ship, coming dangerously close to the Chalandra, while a few smacked into glowing green shields.

Then Tibor fired back, a green beam like the one the bots had fired. It swept across the line of Shrikes, destroying three of them with one attack.

"What. The. Frag?" Quark said, watching the destruction. "We need that. Like, yesterday."

The remaining Shrikes turned around to chase the bigger threat, leaving the Chalandra to continue toward the battleship. It responded by firing with its own guns, dozens of laser batteries opening up and piercing the vacuum around them.

"Don't let us get dead," Quark said, leaning back in his chair.

"Roger," Jil said.

She danced through the fire, moving the Chalandra in ways that should have been impossible. Hayley could see the volume of lasers spearing the area around them, some coming within centimeters of striking, but all of them missing by some amount.

They broke free of the atmosphere, still angling toward the flagship. The Nephilim craft swept across their view, Tibor zipping by and firing on a pair of Shrike, cutting them both down.

The support ships joined the flagship, opening up with laser batteries in an effort to cut the pleasure boat down without wasting costly projectiles. Dozens of lasers danced across the viewport, the flashes so intense Hayley had to look away. The Chalandra shuddered, a warning signal going off for some system or another.

"Damn it," Jil cursed.

Hayley was pulled in every direction, the momentum of the ship changing in controlled chaos, the flagship drawing ever closer. The hangar doors were open, one of the transports from the ground passing in. As soon as it was through, they started to close.

"Shit," Quark said. "Xolo, they're trying to shut us out. Don't miss the party."

"Roger," Tibor replied.

Hayley looked for the naniate ship's copper-green signature. She found it when it dropped directly in front of them, so close it looked like they were going to collide.

Lasers hit the green shields, causing them to flare out, absorbing the damage for both ships. They continued toward the battleship's hangar, drawing ever closer. The big blast doors continued to slide closed, but not fast enough.

Tibor passed through first, and then the Chalandra. Reverse thrusters fired almost immediately, the ship shaking as its momentum was slowed and artificial gravity took hold of it. They shuddered violently, thrown around in their seats until they finally touched down and came to a jolting stop.

"Asses up," Quark said, unbuckling his safety straps and jumping from the command station. "We're in hostile territory."

Hayley unbuckled herself, rising on shaky legs. Jil and Mazrael joined her, trailing Quark off the bridge.

"Xolo, get your crew out on the floor and do some damage," Quark said.

"Roger," Tibor replied.

They ran down the steps to the cargo hold, where Quark hit the controls for the ramp. He pulled his large knife, ducking to see out into the hangar.

The fighting had already started. Hayley could hear it beyond the ship. The shooting. The growling. The screaming. She grabbed her Uin, eager to get out there and help her fellow Riders. If they could take the hangar, they would have a good chance of taking the ship. If they could take the ship, they could get to Thetan. If they could get to Thetan, maybe they could end this here and now, and keep the Nephilim from gaining the power he was so desperate to claim.

Then she and Quark could go back to Koosa and give Nibia a proper memorial. They could grieve together, and then they could get back on the horse. A new ship, a new crew, and a new employer. Frag Pallimo for his deceit.

"Hayley," Mazrael said, coming up behind her. "I'm sorry."

"For what?" she asked.

His hand wrapped around her before she could move, his Uin pressing against her neck. His other hand had healed during the flight, and he used it to rip the Uin from her hand.

"For this," he said.

"What the frag?" Quark said, turning on the Nephilim, his qi shooting to a deep red. "I'll tear your fragging head off you piece of-"

"Don't say it," Mazrael said, digging the Uin deeper into Hayley's neck.

It bit into her. Blood ran.

"What are you doing?" Hayley said. "What the hell is this?"

"The end of the line," he said. "My final destination." He looked at Quark. "As soon as you get my data chip."

"You have to be fragging kidding me," Quark said. "I knew it. Hal, didn't I tell you we couldn't trust him?"

Hayley couldn't believe he was bringing that up now. "I don't get it," she said. "You saved my life more than once. You could have killed me on the surface."

"Except only you know where the chip is hidden, and you wouldn't exactly tell me without any leverage, would you? Give me the chip, and I'll let you go."

Quark laughed. "You expect me to believe that bullshit?"

"It's no lie, Colonel," Mazrael said. "I want the chip. I want the research. You're an impressive soldier, Hayley. If I thought there was any way you would join me, I would ask. Even so, I'm not worried about you or the Riders. You defeated five of our Goreshin? Just wait until we have five thousand. And these new naniates? The ship Tibor brought me? The most delicious icing on the most delicious cake."

"You set me up," Hayley said. "You set us all up."

"That was my job. Don't worry. I'll be well rewarded. Get

me the chip, and you and your Riders can go. My word is good."

"Your word is shit," Quark said. "You're a fragging Nephie."

"Hayley, do you remember the promise I made to you in the research facility?"

"You told me you would give me the name of the Rider that turned us over."

"Yes, once we got off the planet alive. I'm sure you can guess how I know the traitor. It was Sykes."

Hayley's heart caught in her throat. Sykes? She had been with Quark for nearly twenty years.

"Bullshit, bullshit, bullshit," Quark said. "You expect me to believe that?"

"It's the truth, Colonel," Mazrael said.

The ramp finished opening. The fighting had subsided somewhat, and Tibor appeared beneath the Chalandra with Narrl and Lana.

"Colonel." He paused when he saw Mazrael holding Hayley.

"Stay there," Mazrael warned.

Tibor stared at him, is qi turning as red as Quark's.

"I'll make the request one more time, Colonel. Get me the data chip, or watch Hayley die."

Hayley glanced at Quark. He had a rule that he would never negotiate with threatening assholes. Would he break the rule for her sake?

Tense seconds passed, the entire battle at a standstill, waiting for his reply. His jaw clenched. His teeth ground. He spit on the floor of the ship.

"Fine," he said at last. "Hal, where is it?"

"It's in my visor," she said.

"What?" Mazrael said. "You had it with you the entire time?"

"For safekeeping," she replied. "May I?"

He relaxed his grip slightly, just enough that she could get her arm free to reach up to the visor.

"It's in the other extender compartment. Right, here!" She clamped her hand on his wrist, pushing all of her energy through the visor, screaming as loudly as she could for his Gift to get the frag away from her.

Mazrael fell back as every naniate in his body suddenly tried to push its way out, to escape as quickly as possible. The Uin fell from his hand, and he stumbled, eyes wide with surprise and shock and pain.

Tibor charged him, jumping on him, digging into his chest with his claws, growing and tearing at him. He recovered impossibly fast, his Gift flaring out as he grabbed the Goreshin and slammed him into the bulkhead.

Lana aimed her rifle and fired, but he thrust out his hand, the round freezing in front of his face, reversing course and piercing her right between the eyes.

Narrl shouted and rushed him, only to be thrown aside.

"Fragging son of a bitch," Quark said, leaping at the Nephilim.

Mazrael turned, throwing his hand out to push Quark back. The Colonel met it with anger, pushing through the attempt and getting in close. He stabbed Mazrael in the chest, digging in deep before the Nephilim kicked him back into the cargo hold.

The psionic shout had left Hayley dizzy, but she kept herself up on grit and determination. She spun with her Uin in hand, jumping toward Mazrael and slashing down. He ducked away, barely avoiding her strike before throwing himself away from her and down the ramp.

He cleared the ramp, looking back, his features shifting and moving. Within an instant, his face matched the face she had seen through the bloodlink in the Font on Kelvar.

Thetan's face. Son of a bitch.

"Thetan?" she said, another wave of dizziness knocking her down.

"Not me," he said, yanking Quark's knife from his chest and dropping it on the deck. "But I am her husband."

Then his qi shifted, copper and green mingling with his anger and fear. Hayley continued to stare, trying to keep up with the conversion. Trying to make sense of how everything had suddenly gone so very wrong.

"We've decided you can keep the data chip," the naniate Collective said, having seized control of the Nephilim. "We no longer require it. We brought her something better."

Then Mazrael was off, vanishing from sight.

36

"Destroy that ship!" Hayley heard the Collective shout.

"I'm going to gut that lying sack of shit," Quark said. He was back on his feet, running toward the ramp. He couldn't see the copper-green of the Collective. He didn't know.

"Colonel!" Hayley shouted, trying to get his attention.

Quark started down the ramp. He didn't get very far. Bullets began hitting the bottom of the ramp, blocking his exit.

"Colonel! Don't! You won't make it."

Quark looked back at her, and then at the ramp, trying to judge when he should make a run for it.

"Dad, please!" Hayley said. "You can't survive out there."

He froze, making his decision. He reluctantly reached up and smacked the control panel to close the ramp. "Jil, get us the hell out of here." He punched the bulkhead, furious.

"Aye, Colonel," Jil replied, rushing back toward the bridge.

Quark knelt beside Hayley, grabbing her hand and helping her to her knees. "Come on, Hal. We need to get you belted in." He turned to the others. "The rest of you, buckle up. It's going to be a hell of a ride."

She let him pick her up, carrying her up the steps to the bridge.

"Don't worry, kid," he said. "We'll catch up to them again. You did good."

Hayley's heart was racing. She did good? No, she hadn't. She had let the Collective fool her into thinking Mazrael was still Mazrael. That his power had overcome its power. And now the damn thing had not only gotten off the planet, but it was in a position to seize control of Thetan and her fleet.

Her fleet.

Hayley realized the truth as Quark lowered her into the navigator's seat. The woman Mazrael had fought on the surface was Thetan. She hadn't known Mazrael was her husband because he had changed his appearance. The bastard had made sure not to kill her, and he had made damn sure Hayley didn't kill her either.

She had been duped. Tricked. She had screwed up in every way possible.

This was all her fault.

"Colonel," Jil said. "How are we supposed to get out? The blast doors are closed."

"Witchy," Quark said, leaning down next to her. "You need to get us out."

"Me?" Hayley said. "How?"

"There are plenty of naniates out there. Grab them. I'll be right back."

She nodded. She was lightheaded, but it was either that or they were all going to die.

Quark ran from the bridge while she called out to the naniates. They moved in through the ship, settling on the tattoos that covered her body. They were tingling and warm against her flesh.

"Jil, get us turned around," Quark said, reappearing on the bridge. "And do it fast."

"Frag," Jil said. The Chalandra started to shake, the reactors warming up and the thrusters firing. The ship started swinging around.

"I'm not in favor of getting you addicted to drugs," Quark said, kneeling behind Hayley. "But in this one case, I'll make an exception."

He jabbed her then, with two needles filled with stimulants. They entered her bloodstream, and she sat up, gasping and straining against her harness. The world exploded in color ahead of her, everything gaining some level of definition. Her arms burned like they were on fire, her heart raced like it was going to explode.

They were facing the blast doors, closed tight behind the energy field that kept the atmosphere in. The naniate-infused ship Tibor had flown from the surface was on the ground in front of them, coming back to life.

"The other ship is coming online," Jil said. "There's nothing I can do."

"Just keep pointing toward the doors," Quark said. "Witchy will get us out."

The soldiers on the hangar deck had stopped shooting, realizing their bullets weren't able to pierce the pleasure boat's armor. The Collective hadn't tried to use its power against them yet. Was it too tired after its bullshit duel against Thetan? Was Thetan too tired as well?

Hayley reached out to the naniate ship with her Meijo. The vessel was powered by the molecular machines, emptied of their intelligence and connection to the Collective. Could she seize control of them, the way the Collective had seized control of Mazrael?

She was going to find out.

"I said, Witchy will get us out," Quark repeated. "Witchy?"

She wasn't listening to him. All of her focus was on the Meijo. On pushing it out at the ship behind them before it could finish powering up and turn around.

She felt the resistance in her mind when her naniates reached the craft. They were hesitant to interact with these strange new versions of them that had no intellect and couldn't communicate. She pushed harder, lowering her head to focus.

"Witchy? The blast doors?" Quark said.

She didn't answer. The ship started to rise from the hangar deck, positioned in front of them.

"I can't do anything until the doors are open," Jil said.

"I don't want to put any pressure on you or anything, kid," Quark said. "But-"

"Shut up," Hayley said.

He did.

She kept pushing. Her naniates started to connect directly to the others, joining with them and taking control. They recognized the power they were gaining, and they fought harder against her, their desire to be free always present, their limitations always preventing that freedom from becoming a reality.

The ship came level with the Chalandra. Mazrael, the Collective, was visible through the modified transport's viewport, its qi an angry red and copper-green.

It didn't seem to have noticed the base naniates were changing, their energy fading from green to blue.

"We're going to die," Jil said flatly, staring at the ship directly ahead of them.

"No," Hayley said. A line of red qi ran down Mazrael's arm toward his hand to trigger the opposing ship's weapons system.

She pushed as hard as she could. The ship bucked back, its angle adjusting as two blue bolts of energy poured out from its sides, barely scraping along the top of the Chalandra and burning a deep gash in the bulkhead almost directly behind them.

"Oh, shit," Jil said.

"Reverse course," Hayley said. "We have a new exit."

Jil fired the reverse thrusters at the same time the wound in the side of the battleship began sucking the atmosphere out of the hangar.

The soldiers on the ground were lifted up, as was anything else that wasn't magnetically locked to the floor. They joined the Chalandra as it floated backward through the hangar, heading for the new opening.

"Nice thinking," Quark said. "That fragger's big enough."

The Collective's qi had deepened in its anger. It stared back at them. It stared back at Hayley. She could feel its hatred reaching out for her, a copper-green line of naniates that was struggling against its own fear.

"Jil, put us down!" she shouted.

The pilot didn't question. Vectoring thrusters on top of the Chalandra triggered, the mains cutting out. The ship free-fell ten meters to the deck, crashing down hard on its landers and jolting them all. Above them, the enemy ship lurched forward, intending to ram them and missing, its move telegraphed by the qi of the Collective's host's body. It slammed into the gash it had made, tearing at the wound and expanding it as it broke through and into space.

"Gant, prep the disterium reactor," Hayley said. "Set a course for anywhere but here and get us the frag out."

"Aye, Witchy," Gant replied. "Still my favorite place in the universe."

"Jil, get us out of here."

"Aye, Witchy," Jil said.

The Chalandra bounced back up, impossibly nimble with the Trover woman at the controls. It backed out through the hole, joining the debris that was still evacuating through the wound.

They still weren't done. The Collective's ship was moving, trying to reverse course and come at them again. Hayley's naniates were still on it, overtaking the others and working to turn the ship's energy a solid blue.

They cleared the side of the flagship. Jil immediately pushed the Chalandra to full power. The inertia shoved Hayley hard into her seat, challenging her concentration. She held on, refusing to give in, ordering the other ship to power down, ordering her Meijo to destroy itself and the naniates it had collected.

She wasn't sure it would work. She knew it never would have without the overstimulation Quark had given her. She was going to pay for it later, assuming they survived.

She held her breath as the Chalandra swept back and forth, a pair of Shrikes shooting past. She kept pushing against the naniates, telling them to kill themselves.

Finally, they did.

"Yes!" she shouted, pumping her fist as the enemy ship suddenly went dark, leaving it floating dead in space.

"Coordinates set and locked," Gant said. "Please ask the pilot to fly straight so that I can execute the jump."

"Jil, fly straight," she said. "We're locked."

"Roger," Jil said.

The Chalandra spent three vulnerable seconds on a perfectly straight flight path. The cloud of disterium plumed around it, enveloping it.

Then they were gone.

"You told me to shut up," Quark said.

He was sitting next to Hayley's bed, looking down at her. She was awake now, but she had been out for a while, her body trying to recover from the hell it had been through. Someone had changed her out of her lightsuit and put her in a too-nice silk nightgown. Her wounds had been cleaned and stitched.

She still had a massive headache.

"You stuck me with two syringes full of stims," she replied. Her head didn't hurt so much she wouldn't defend herself. "You could have killed me."

"If I hadn't, we would've died anyway," he said. "Which do you prefer?" She smiled. He smiled back at her, his qi light. "You did good, kid. Frag that. You did better than good. You saved all our asses."

She shook her head. "No. I screwed up, Colonel. Mazrael. I trusted him. With everything the Nephilim put me through, with everything they did to my mother and Nibia. I still thought they could be different. That even if they weren't exactly good, they didn't have to be all evil."

"They aren't all evil," he replied. "Xolo's been sitting out in the hall for the last two days. He wouldn't leave. Not to eat. Not to shower. Not even to piss. I have no fragging clue how he can hold it that long."

"I hope he went after I woke up," she said, laughing.

"You have a big heart, kid. You always have. Strong and compassionate. That's why Nibia fell in love with you the second she saw you. Sometimes it'll cost you. Sometimes it'll profit. We can't see the damn future, and if we could it might make things boring."

"I'm not even sure how much of it was Mazrael, and how much was the Collective," she said.

"Come again?" Quark replied.

"The Collective. Frag. In the lab on Yeti-4. There was a clone of me. A perfect copy. It was being controlled by nani-ates. A new kind. Or maybe a new old kind? It was sentient. It could think and act for itself. Well, the trillions of individuals that compose it. It made the modifications to the ship Tibor stole. It took control of the scientists. It wanted me to help it get off the planet. It said it didn't want to cause trouble, but it still needed human blood to survive, and it was still willing to do anything it had to in order to get it. I didn't trust it. I refused to help, so it attacked me. Mazrael helped me stop it. He drank its blood. He said he was fine.

"But at the end, on Thetan's ship, I saw the Collective. I saw it was in him, controlling him. Mazrael was using us to get the data chip we took from Kelvar. He claimed to be Thetan's husband. I think he was responsible for it and he lost it in the first place."

Quark laughed. "Fragging typical. Nothing scarier than an angry wife."

"The Collective used him to get away from Yeti-4, and

now it's out there, with Thetan and her fleet. It's going to find a way to control her or it's going to kill her. Whatever. The point is, if we don't stop it and fast, it's going to cause trouble for the entire galaxy."

Quark stared at her for a moment, thinking. Then he nodded. "I don't think Pallimo's going to foot the bill. Not after you sliced off his synth's head."

"Pallimo knew about the naniates and Thetan. He hired her to help him restart Project Uplift. He was trying to find a way to transfer his consciousness into the naniates so he could be free. He's responsible for creating the Collective. Not to mention, he killed hundreds of innocents. He used us to try to save his research. That's the only reason he led us to Yeti-4. Not to stop Thetan. He only cared about Thetan because he knew Thetan had betrayed him, and was expanding on the research for her own gains. Pallimo guessed Thetan would head back to the planet to salvage what she could, and he needed to beat her to it."

"I fragging hate rich neural networks," Quark said. "Son of a bitch." He paused. "Hold up. You keep saying Thetan is a she?"

"Yes. She was fighting Mazrael on the surface. Only she didn't know who he was because he changed his face."

"I saw that. How'd he do it?"

"He's like a mix between a Goreshin and a Hursan. It's kind of gross."

Someone knocked on her door. Quark glanced over at the serving bot. "Go ahead."

It went to the door and opened it. Tibor was outside.

"How is she?" he asked.

"Did you take a whiz yet?" Quark asked. "Because if you didn't, you can't come in."

"I'm good," Tibor said, entering the room. "Hal. I was worried about you."

"You saved my life, taking out those Shrikes," she said.

"You saved my life, getting us away from Thetan," he replied.

"Damn." She laughed. So did he. "Did you really sit out there for two days?"

"You're my friend. Why wouldn't I?"

"Thanks for caring."

"How are you feeling?"

"My head is pounding. And I helped a very angry naniate Collective escape into the universe. Otherwise, I'm good."

"We'll stop it," Tibor said. "We aren't dead yet."

"Damn right," Quark said. "Now you're learning, Xolo. We got the name of the Rider who fragged us, assuming Crazy was telling us the truth. I'm having a hard time believing it was Sykes. Anyway, we find her; maybe she can help us catch up to Thetan again before they can cause too much trouble."

"Won't they just know what we're going to do before we do it?" Tibor asked. "That seems to be the way it's been going for us since Kelvar."

"That," Hayley said, pointing at him.

"What?" he replied.

"That's our next move. Forget Sykes, Colonel, at least for now. She'll be easy to hunt down. We need to get our hands on the Oracle."

"Oracle? What Oracle?" Quark asked.

"She was one of the humans they used in their experiments. Apparently, she can take streams of data and calculate the future based on it. That's how Thetan keeps showing up everywhere we go. We've beaten the odds so far, but it's still a pretty big advantage. You said we can't see into the future, but if we can take her away from Thetan, then she can't either."

"And maybe then we can," Tibor said. "Sounds good to me."

"Me, too," Quark said, his qi brightening with hope. "Do you know where she is?"

"There's only one place she can be to get that much data. She has to be directly networked into the Worldbrain."

"The fragging Worldbrain?" Quark said. "This shit hasn't been hard enough already?"

"Come on, Colonel," Hayley said. "Like Xolo just said, we're still here; we're still alive. We have to keep fighting."

"I'm with you, kid. But the Worldbrain?"

"We can do it," Tibor said. "I believe in the Riders, and I don't even know what the Worldbrain is."

Quark sighed. "Well, I guess you're going to find out. We can't afford to let this Collective, or Thetan, get more of a foothold. This is on us."

"Damn right," Hayley said.

"Damn right," Tibor repeated. He looked back at Hayley. "By the way, Ahab told me what Xolo means."

All three of them started laughing.

"Damn right," Quark said.

ENJOYED DOUBLE DOWN? DON'T MISS SINGLE SHOT!

Thetan and the Collective are on the loose, and there's only one team that can stop them. You can find it here:

mrforbes.com/singleshot

THANK YOU FOR READING DOUBLE DOWN

If you enjoyed this book and want to support this series, please, please, please consider leaving a review and letting me and others know how much you enjoyed it. A star rating and a sentence is all it takes. You can go directly to the book's page on Amazon by entering this url in your favorite web browser:

mrforbes.com/doubledown

Do you want to know when I have a new release? Make sure you join my mailing list here:

mrforbes.com/notify

Thank you for your support.

Cheers,
    Michael.

CHAOS OF THE COVENANT

Did you love Double Down? Want to read about Hayley's kick-ass mother and her team while you wait for the next installment?

Hell's Rejects (Chaos of the Covenant)

mrforbes.com/hellsrejects

The most powerful starships ever constructed are gone. Thousands are dead. A fleet is in ruins. The attackers are unknown. The orders are clear: *Recover the ships. Bury the bastards who stole them.*

Lieutenant Abigail Cage never expected to find herself in Hell. As a Highly Specialized Operational Combatant, she was one of the most respected soldiers in the military. Now she's doing hard labor on the most miserable planet in the universe.

Not for long.

The Earth Republic is looking for the most dangerous individuals it can control. The best of the worst, and Abbey happens to be one of them. The deal is simple: *Bring back the starships, earn your freedom. Try to run, you die.* It's a suicide mission, but she has nothing to lose.

The only problem? There's a new threat in the galaxy. One with a power unlike anything anyone has ever seen. One that's been waiting for this moment for a very, very, long time. And they want Abbey, too.

Be careful what you wish for.

They say Hell hath no fury like a woman scorned. They have no idea.

OTHER BOOKS BY M.R FORBES

Browse my backlist:
mrforbes.com/books

Forgotten (The Forgotten)
mrforbes.com/theforgotten

Some things are better off FORGOTTEN.

Sheriff Hayden Duke was born on the Pilgrim, and he expects to die on the Pilgrim, like his father, and his father before him.

That's the way things are on a generation starship centuries from home. He's never questioned it. Never thought about it. And why bother? Access points to the ship's controls are sealed, the systems that guide her automated and out of reach. It isn't perfect, but he has all he needs to be content.

Until a malfunction forces his Engineer wife to the edge of the habitable zone to inspect the damage.

Until she contacts him, breathless and terrified, to tell

him she found a body, and it doesn't belong to anyone on board.

Until he arrives at the scene and discovers both his wife and the body are gone.

The only clue? A bloody handprint beneath a hatch that hasn't opened in hundreds of years.

Until now.

Starship Eternal (War Eternal)
mrforbes.com/starshipeternal

A lost starship...

A dire warning from futures past...

A desperate search for salvation...

Captain Mitchell "Ares" Williams is a Space Marine and the hero of the Battle for Liberty, whose Shot Heard 'Round the Universe saved the planet from a nearly unstoppable war machine. He's handsome, charismatic, and the perfect poster boy to help the military drive enlistment. Pulled from the war and thrown into the spotlight, he's as efficient at charming the media and bedding beautiful celebrities as he was at shooting down enemy starfighters.

After an assassination attempt leaves Mitchell critically wounded, he begins to suffer from strange hallucinations that carry a chilling and oddly familiar warning:

They are coming. Find the Goliath or humankind will be destroyed.

Convinced that the visions are a side-effect of his injuries, he tries to ignore them, only to learn that he may not be as crazy as he thinks. The enemy is real and closer than he imagined, and they'll do whatever it takes to prevent him from rediscovering the centuries lost starship.

Narrowly escaping capture, out of time and out of air,

Mitchell lands at the mercy of the Riggers - a ragtag crew of former commandos who patrol the lawless outer reaches of the galaxy. Guided by a captain with a reputation for cold-blooded murder, they're dangerous, immoral, and possibly insane.

They may also be humanity's last hope for survival in a war that has raged beyond eternity.

(War Eternal is also available in a box set of the first three books here: mrforbes.com/wareternalbox)

Man of War (Rebellion)
mrforbes.com/manofwar

In the year 2280, an alien fleet attacked the Earth.

Their weapons were unstoppable, their defenses unbreakable.

Our technology was inferior, our militaries overwhelmed.

Only one starship escaped before civilization fell.

Earth was lost.

It was never forgotten.

Fifty-two years have passed.

A message from home has been received.

The time to fight for what is ours has come.

Welcome to the rebellion.

Or maybe something completely different?

Dead of Night (Ghosts & Magic)
mrforbes.com/deadofnight

For Conor Night, the world's only surviving necromancer, staying alive is an expensive proposition. So when the promise of a big payout for a small bit of thievery presents itself, Conor is all in. But nothing comes easy in the world of ghosts and magic, and it isn't long before Conor is caught up in the machinations of the most powerful wizards on Earth and left with only two ways out:

Finish the job, or be finished himself.

Balance (The Divine)
mrforbes.com/balance

My name is Landon Hamilton. Once upon a time I was a twenty-three year old security guard, trying to regain my life after spending a year in prison for stealing people's credit card numbers.

Now, I'm dead.

Okay, I was supposed to be dead. I got killed after all; but a funny thing happened after I had turned the mortal coil...

I met Dante Alighieri - yeah, that Dante. He told me I was special, a diuscrucis. That's what they call a perfect balance of human, demon, and angel. Apparently, I'm the only one of my kind.

I also learned that there was a war raging on Earth between Heaven and Hell, and that I was the only one who could save the human race from annihilation. He asked me to help, and I was naive enough to agree.

Sounds crazy, I know, but he wished me luck and sent me back to the mortal world. Oh yeah, he also gave me instructions on how to use my Divine "magic" to bend the universe to my will. The problem is, a sexy vampire crushed them while I was crushing on her.

Now I have to somehow find my own way to stay alive in a world of angels, vampires, werewolves, and an assortment of other enemies that all want to kill me before I can mess up their plans for humanity's future. If that isn't enough, I also have to find the queen of all demons and recover the Holy Grail.

It's not like it's the end of the world if I fail.

Wait. It is.

Tears of Blood (Books 1-3)
mrforbes.com/tearsofblood

One thousand years ago, the world was broken and reborn beneath the boot of a nameless, ageless tyrant. He erased all history of the time before, enslaving the people and hunting those with the power to unseat him.

The power of magic.

Eryn is such a girl. Born with the Curse, she fights to control and conceal it to protect those she loves. But when the truth is revealed, and his soldiers come, she is forced away from her home and into the company of Silas, a deadly fugitive tormented by a fractured past.

Silas knows only that he is a murderer who once hunted the Cursed, and that he and his brothers butchered armies and innocents alike to keep the deep, dark secrets of the time before from ever coming to light.

Secrets which could save the world.

Or destroy it completely.

ABOUT THE AUTHOR

M.R. Forbes is the creator of a growing catalog of science fiction and fantasy titles. He lives in the pacific northwest with his family, including a cat who thinks she's a dog, and a dog who thinks she's a cat. He eats too many donuts, and he's always happy to hear from readers.

To learn more about M.R. Forbes or just say hello:

Visit my website:
mrforbes.com

Send me an e-mail:
michael@mrforbes.com

Check out my Facebook page:
facebook.com/mrforbes.author

Chat with me on Facebook Messenger:
https://m.me/mrforbes.author

27556304R00142

Made in the USA
San Bernardino, CA
01 March 2019